I've travelled the world twice over,
Met the famous: saints and sinners,
Poets and artists, kings and queens,
Old stars and hopeful beginners,
I've been where no-one's been before,
Learned secrets from writers and cooks
All with one library ticket
To the wonderful world of books.

© JANICE JAMES.

JOURNEY NO MORE

Losing confidence in the validity and future of her relationship with the man she is engaged to marry, Joanne Kirkham leaves her safe job as an interpreter to become a travel courier in Europe. Her Swiss driver, Hans Lindt, saps her confidence at the very outset and subsequently proves to be a perplexing companion. When accidents and mishaps threaten the travel company and endanger Hans, Joanne finds herself plunging ever deeper into an atmosphere of apprehension, mistrust and danger.

KAY STEPHENS

JOURNEY NO MORE

Complete and Unabridged

ULVERSCROFT
Leicester

First published 1978 by
William Collins Sons & Co Ltd.
London

First Large Print Edition
published February 1983
by arrangement with
Collins, London & Glasgow

British Library CIP Data

Stephens, Kay
Journey no more.—Large print ed.
(Ulverscroft large print series: romance)
I. Title
823'.914[F]   PR6069.T/

ISBN 0-7089-0925-6

Published by
F. A. Thorpe (Publishing) Ltd.
Anstey, Leicestershire
Printed and Bound in Great Britain by
T. J. Press (Padstow) Ltd., Padstow, Cornwall

Love is
a time of enchantment:
in it all days are fair and all fields
green. Youth is blest by it,
old age made benign: the eyes of love see
roses blooming in December,
and sunshine through rain. Verily
is the time of true-love
a time of enchantment—and
Oh! how eager is woman
to be bewitched!

1

DAPPLED clouds chased each other towards distant Alpine peaks. Shading her eyes against the sun, Joanne detected the silver speck which was the plane they awaited.

"Here she comes!" Stella exclaimed, then laughed; "Feel you want to turn and run?"

Joanne grimaced. "How did you know?"

"Come and meet Hans—he'd arrive with the party going out on that one. You've time to get acquainted before your mob clears Customs."

Stella smiled as Joanne fell into step beside her. "Don't look so scared! Remember they don't know you're our new courier—unless you give it away—and you won't if you cope the way you have with me this fortnight."

Passing the terminal's glass doors, Joanne sensed somebody watching them. She glanced back. The solitary man in a white safari suit turned on his heel.

Touching her arm, Stella indicated several coaches in the now-familiar green and gold, parked with others of diverse colours. She hesitated, then nodded towards the third in line: "That'll be Hans . . ." Joanne saw no one—until they were nearer. Then she observed long legs by the driver's door. The rest of him remained concealed.

"Hallo there, Hans—long time no see!" Stella greeted him.

With a Germanic mumble which escaped Joanne, the young man straightened his back and glanced round.

"Oh—hallo, Stella." His voice was deep, heavily accented. "Some fool tourist has overturned that ridiculous amount of change we carry for road tolls and so on! Naturally, he did not help to retrieve it!"

Stella made sympathetic noises, which Hans chose to ignore. He was staring, disdainfully, at Joanne.

"Who is she?" he enquired of Stella. Joanne felt indignant colour rising. She might be new, but she wasn't a deaf mute!

"Your courier—Joanne Kirkham. Joanne, this is Hans Lindt . . ." and after a fractional hesitation, Stella added, hastily, "your driver this trip."

His eyes seemed wary. He snorted; no smile warmed the suntanned features while, *again*, he scrutinized Joanne: "Hope she's well-trained!"

"I've done my best," Stella began, eyes dancing, "I'm sure you'll find . . ."

". . . she is helpless, and I have to do the job for her!"

Still unsmiling, Hans turned away: "I did not know I was being burdened with a beginner."

Stella looked up as the plane circled, prior to landing: "You'd better dash, Joanne—Hans will see to your case . . ."

"Already it is starting, yes?" he demanded. "Soon, she must accustom herself to humping many suitcases, not to leave for me the hard work."

"Go on," Stella retorted, undaunted, "you love demonstrating your strength!"

As the two girls retraced their steps to the airport building, Stella grinned: "Well, best of luck—you're on your own now."

Joanne made a face: "Even more than I expected—by the sound of Hans! Is he always so abominably rude?"

Stella laughed, "That's just his way—till you get to know him. Hans is all right, really."

"He had me fooled!"

3

"You'll see—he'll turn out better than you imagine! Well, love, I must leave you to it—I've ten minutes to freshen up before my flight to Antwerp."

Feeling conspicuous and isolated, Joanne stood by the lockers to one side of the momentarily deserted arrival lounge. She patted her short brown hair nervously—hoping the eyes that matched weren't betraying her recent sleeplessness.

Whatever had possessed her to throw up a perfectly good job as an interpreter—a job she'd understood and liked—for the hectic, mid-season life of a travel courier?

"With boorish strangers!" she added, silently.

Joanne caught herself twisting the engagement ring she'd so nearly returned that disastrous week-end James went coaching the rowing crew, leaving her with his parents. She sighed. His increasing indifference towards her had driven her from England—and until this separation proved to both of them that marriage would be right for them, she was not returning.

"Miss Kirkham?" The smiling ground-hostess interrupted her thoughts. "Your tourists are claiming baggage now—will be here shortly."

Joanne smiled back—as if practising for her clients—and adjusted her badge.

Mr. and Mrs. Hughes, an elderly couple, bustled towards her. While she checked their names against the schedule, a group congregated, chattering eagerly, excitedly. Joanne had to remind them to stand aside and leave room for others coming in on the flight. One family kept them waiting, but soon she was leading everyone to the coach, explaining *en route* (on Stella's advice) the seat numbering.

Her initial hurdle surmounted, she was breathing more easily as she slid back the door.

"Did you get them lost?" Hans questioned, consulting his watch. Ignoring the remark, Joanne gave him, curtly, the number of cases for loading, then concentrated on organizing people into their seats.

Leaving the airport for the Basle suburbs, she introduced herself and Hans, over the mike. He, she observed, raised a hand in cheery salute. Why couldn't he extend his friendliness towards herself? Were his amiable moments sufficiently rare to be rationed?

Once beyond the city, with its places of interest requiring commentary, Joanne lit a cigarette.

"Don't I get one?" demanded a voice to her left.

She threw Hans a glance.

"It is usual—most couriers prefer that I keep one hand on the wheel!" When she hesitated still, he said, scathingly, "Stop worrying, I contribute my share of cigarettes!"

Joanne inhaled deeply, picked up her pack and lit a cigarette for him, handing it across when the road ahead was clear.

"Thanks." Unexpectedly, Hans grinned. "Pleasant flavour—this lipstick!"

Joanne gave him a sidelong look—maybe he would prove human, fleetingly!

She watched the road, thinking back over the procedure to date; pretty sure she hadn't forgotten anything—yet. The difficulty was remembering everything, whilst remaining alert to their clients' needs.

She hated feeling so raw. For five years, since leaving school at eighteen, she'd become gradually conversant with her work.

Today, she felt like a schoolgirl again, starting a new school!

"You're supposed to give them some gen on that mountain, over to the right," Hans hissed, in German.

"*Danke*," Joanne replied, reaching for the mike, wondering whether he was being helpful—or enjoyed picking on her.

★　★　★

Early evening traffic through Lucerne delayed them. Joanne knew they'd arrive late at their hotel. That wouldn't please either travel-weary passengers or hotel staff.

Hans alone appeared unperturbed. When she consulted the clock again, he sighed: "Stop fidgeting—you'll not get us there any sooner. Tell them something about the place, keep their minds off the time. And you have not recommended wines to accompany their meal—nor explained the currency . . ."

"Here . . . !" She gestured with the mike. "Since you know it all!"

"Not my line—and I was only trying to help."

Something told her this could be true.

"Okay, I'm sorry."

7

Joanne noticed his lips twitching slightly. "A rare woman—who can apologize!" he remarked, in German again, then concentrated, silently, on the antics of the car they followed.

Arrival at the hotel and allocating rooms went smoothly; although Joanne had to endure Hans's complaint that she sorted luggage too slowly.

There was time only for a quick wash before going down to dinner, but she managed to be in the panelled dining-room before the first of her party. When she observed Hans crossing to the corner table she realized she was heading for two weeks of meals shared with his unpredictability.

As she joined him, Hans gave a curt nod, without interrupting his progress with the soup. Joanne decided she ought to make conversation—if only to keep up appearances. No one would enjoy a relaxed holiday with antagonism between driver and courier.

"You're German then?"

"Swiss!" he corrected sharply, indicating a major blunder.

"Sorry," she murmured, thankful the waiter's arrival excused further comment.

"I live nearby to Berne, was thirty last

birthday, and my hobby is skiing—anything else?" Hans disarmed her with a glint of laughter in his blue eyes.

Joanne allowed herself to smile. "You've robbed me of the only topic of conversation!"

Hans regarded her steadily. "Certainly the only one of interest!"

So—he dismissed her as boring! Or . . . was he baiting her? Her sudden, wild urge to test this theory was shelved as a young woman approached their table.

"Er—Joanne," she began. "It's this soup—my husband doesn't eat mushroom . . ."

Joanne stood up and, turning, looked about for a waiter. Aware of Hans's eyes boring into her back, she straightened her shoulders. She'd show him she could cope with every problem. Even though these had begun before she was ready.

★　★　★

Breakfast next morning, the first continental breakfast for many of their group, was no easier. But Joanne (having slept through sheer exhaustion) felt able to tackle anything. Besides, Stella had forewarned her about people who were accustomed to eggs and bacon for breakfast while on holiday. She was unprepared, nevertheless, for Mr. and Mrs. Hughes's objection to being relegated to the third floor, whilst younger couples had rooms on the first.

Sympathizing, Joanne decided to check accommodation schedules for subsequent nights and re-shuffle discreetly.

After the overnight stop, everyone was rested and cheerful as they wound their way over the impressive St. Gotthard pass into Italy. Hans had tossed Joanne a cigarette pack and—so far—she'd remembered to keep him supplied.

Nearing the Italian border, he glanced across: "Just tell them to have their passports ready, and leave everything to me. I know the drill, and most of the officers know me."

He was as good as his word and they were soon on their way again. Joanne felt she owed him a "thank you". Hans chuckled: "You will not go far astray doing as I tell you!" She didn't fancy two weeks of obeying him but, lacking experience, couldn't dissent. She might need somebody who knew the ropes.

They drew off the Autostrada for a break, which Joanne spent sorting Italian change for her clients. At last she hastily drained her tepid coffee before emerging to a molten world of heat shimmering from concrete.

Hans, at the wheel again, was drumming impatiently on its rim. He indicated his watch and jerked his head towards the rear. Two seats were vacant. Joanne ran her eyes over the remaining faces . . . Tom something, wasn't it—the tall, dark, young man with laughing eyes, and his companion, Henry O'Brien?

"Go and get them," Hans instructed, in German—as though he were speaking to a child of nine.

Joanne returned to the building. She looked round the bar and in the supermarket, finding nobody she recognized. Frowning, she looked towards the toilets . . . Well, she couldn't investigate there!

As she rejoined the coach, Hans raised an eyebrow.

"I think they must be in the . . ." she began.

"So?"

"Couldn't *you* . . . I mean—would you go and look?" She hated asking him—hated even more his contemptuous glare as he left with an exaggerated sigh.

When he reappeared, laughing and talking

amiably with their missing passengers, Joanne was infuriated.

"Your job to round them up, *Liebchen*," Hans hissed, his smile freezing once they were mobile. "You must stop playing the innocent, and dive in anywhere!"

They stayed the night at a drab town in Northern Italy which, it being Sunday, lacked entertainment. Spotting Hans's fair head in the bar after dinner, Joanne decided on a walk.

It was pleasantly cool and, meeting first the MacDonalds, the family who had kept them waiting at the airport, then the Johnsons who'd had problems with the soup, she warmed to their delight in greeting her.

"Care for a night-cap, Joanne?" A voice called as, eventually, she returned to the hotel. Tom. "As a peace-offering?"

"Thanks, I will—but I mustn't stay long." She accompanied him to the bar, noticing that Hans, as well as Henry, was still there. Surprisingly, Hans found her a stool.

After the drink, Joanne smiled. "Thank you—but I must turn in now."

"So soon?" Hans protested. Joanne suspected mockery, but his eyes, meeting hers, revealed nothing.

She went to bed, nevertheless, acutely aware that he disturbed her. She believed, too, that his changed attitude had been calculated towards that end!

* * *

Next morning, able to recall the names of everyone in the party, Joanne began to relax. She'd gained confidence, for thus far there had been no major catastrophe, and—at last—Hans seemed . . . friendly.

Her relief evaporated over breakfast. His blue eyes were veiled as he grunted a response to her greeting. And during their coffee break, he appeared so preoccupied Joanne felt compelled to ask what was wrong.

He frowned, sought her eyes briefly, and sighed. "Nothing that will affect my driving of this coach." Which seemed to preclude further comment.

But it didn't end Joanne's concern. Repeatedly, she caught herself watching him, wishing he hadn't excluded her so pointedly. She knew all about having some worry—if he let her get through to him, she might begin to understand, and perhaps be of some help.

She pondered, ruefully—hadn't she problems

enough? She'd not yet heard from James, his letter should await her in Rome. And she couldn't even guess what he might say.

Joanne sighed, remembering. James had adopted a semi-humorous tolerance since that row at his mother's. He'd accepted her explanation that she must get away and re-think her life, but if she'd subconsciously hoped he'd bring forward their wedding instead she'd been disappointed. And whilst he'd seemed happy to have her address in Rome, he'd avoided committing himself to writing frequently, saying, "There are lots of events in the Rowing Calendar, I'll be busy . . ."

Joanne was bewildered still, for though James had drawn her to him for a lingering kiss at the airport she hadn't felt reassured. What was happening to them? Ever since she'd met James, years ago, he'd only had to hold her close to convince her everything would be all right. Had the magic of their relationship disintegrated?

"You don't look exactly carefree yourself!" Hans jolted her back to the present. "You see, I'm not totally disinterested," he added, below the engine's hum.

Joanne managed a grin. "Problems won't prevent *me* from doing my job either!"

14

"At which you're proving efficient," he responded, surprising her yet again.

"Never expected that from you!" she exclaimed, lapsing into the German they used for private conversation *en route*.

"Ah, but you have delighted me. I know I was unfair to you at first . . ."

Hans hesitated. When Joanne glanced sideways he was looking straight ahead, but he gave a tiny shrug. "Things were . . . going badly . . ." he sighed. "You may as well know—your predecessor had given me a piece of her mind, because we didn't see eye to eye. The girl was no use—I've been blessed with a succession of imbeciles all season—but my . . . *the* office hadn't even told me you'd replaced her."

"Are you so fussy then, that they have to let you choose your own couriers?"

The remark appeared to throw him. He took a quick breath, she noticed, before replying. "Well, I prefer someone who uses their intelligence!"

She could only assume that included her, and smiled in acknowledgement.

★   ★   ★

Arriving in Rome, Joanne had to wait through allocating rooms, sorting baggage, and handing in passports, before opening the envelope with familiar handwriting. Crossing to the lift, she smoothed out the single notepaper.

Dear Joanne,

How are things? They are fine with me. Having a marvellous time. Do you remember Helen? We met her at York Regatta last year. Bumped into her at Henley—we're seeing quite a bit of each other. She has a flat in Town, these days . . .

Her eyes misted—already someone was taking her place. Somebody else was accompanying James to their favourite haunts . . . Recalling Helen's elegance at York Regatta Ball, Joanne swallowed hard. James would never treat *her* casually.

At the lift gates, Joanne collided with Hans who was busy with the last few suitcases. He steadied her, seemed about to speak, but changed his mind. She went to her room to read the rest of James's wretched letter.

* * *

That evening they were giving their clients

the "Rome by Night" tour; Joanne forced herself to concentrate on all she'd swotted up about places of interest. Consequently, she'd no time even to think about James until, leaving her party admiring the Trevi fountain, she made for the bar frequented by her colleagues. Although the Company had a large fleet of coaches there was, she'd discovered, a pleasing fellowship between its employees.

Hans, on seeing her, left the group he was with and beckoned her to a corner table. He ordered her drink, smiled—kindly, she thought, then enquired: "Not bad news, I hope, from home?"

When Joanne didn't reply, he persisted: "That letter—I could not ignore your expression."

She sighed, longing to confide, wishing Hans was the sort she'd have chosen to confide in.

"Well, it wasn't good news," she responded, briefly, and was stupidly disappointed when he assumed that closed the subject. What did she want—why be upset by his lack of interest?

Returning, late, to their hotel, they found the street jammed with parked vehicles. Hans set down their passengers away from the kerb.

"Now what happens about the coach?" Joanne asked. He snorted: "I cruise around, park as near as possible—*if* there is some space into which I can squeeze her!"

"Would I be any use directing you into a tight spot?"

"Of course—but I should warn you it could be more than a few metres walk back here."

"Never mind," she answered, and caught his smile.

Walking, eventually, towards the hotel, Hans took her arm. "I wasn't prying, earlier. You've enough on—coping first time round, without worrying about anything else."

"Thanks." She hated the chill in her voice.

He consulted his watch: "The bar will be closed now—against such eventualities, I carry a bottle or two. You can join me if you like—upstairs."

She started to refuse and Hans laughed. "Only for a drink!" he added. Seeing him glance at her hands, she discovered she was twisting her engagement ring again. She forced her hand to her shoulder-bag and smiled. "Why not—thank you."

"Take a seat . . ." Inside his room, Hans

18

indicated the one comfortable chair and took bottles from the wardrobe. "Cinzano—or whisky?"

Joanne chose Cinzano and watched as Hans found glasses. He threw himself down on the bed, lit a cigarette and offered them to her.

She shook her head. "I smoke more than enough."

"Nerves?"

"In a way."

"Hazards of taking this on in mid-season—or boy-friend trouble?" He evidently believed in the direct approach.

"Both, I suppose . . ." Joanne hesitated, longing again to confide—wondering, still, why—for she didn't particularly like this man.

Suddenly, scruples vanishing, she was telling him, ". . . and so I came away, to . . . decide if he's the one."

His expression inscrutable, Hans was studying her, but having started, she couldn't keep anything back, not how desolate she'd felt when James left her with his parents, nor how small amongst his acquaintances. She expected Hans to remark how childish this all sounded, but he only laughed, ruefully, "Seems we both have troubles . . ."

19

"And yours?"

He shrugged. "Domestic," he said, hastily, before changing the subject. "I decided the other day to invite you for a drink—because the antagonism was . . . well, rather noticeable. I'm not sure, *now*, that I need say anything but we can clear the air . . ." He glanced across and Joanne observed that her smile had surprised him. He hesitated, nonplussed, "Oh—forget it."

"No—go on."

He smiled, too, and inhaled: "It was only— when we were constantly bickering—I realized that it mustn't continue. Since I'm . . . the old-stager, I should make some effort. Maybe you are under too much pressure one way and another. I'll try to make allowances—but let us not snarl so readily, eh?"

Joanne nodded, uncertain what to say.

"So—shall we concentrate on ensuring our clients have an enjoyable holiday?" he insisted.

"Sure," Joanne agreed, rising to go. "With a pact to remind each other, without offence, if we forget."

"Fine." He frowned, watching her head for the door: "Going already?"

"I'm afraid I'm tired."

20

Hans came to her, placed a hand on her arm—sending electric sparks coursing through her: "Glad you haven't taken offence now."

Joanne scrutinized his expression. "You're utterly committed to the Company, aren't you—also to the well-being of its clients!"

His eyes registered secret amusement, though his lips didn't even smile.

"*Jawohl*," he responded, gravely, opening the door for her.

* * * I/404390

For Joanne the next morning was free, since a local guide was escorting their party to St. Peter's, the Forum and the Colosseum. She forced herself to answer James's letter and, somehow, the task proved less difficult than she'd expected. There was plenty to relate; her experiences since leaving England, the places she had visited.

Reading through the completed letter, Joanne discovered she'd devoted a whole page to Hans, who emerged sounding more agreeable than her initial dislike would have indicated.

Addressing the envelope, she smiled to

herself; perhaps a little competition would be good for James.

Unfortunately, *en route* for Sorrento, where they were spending the following week, Hans reverted to moroseness.

Joanne was annoyed, recalling everything he'd said only last night. Today, his only acknowledgement of her was the frequent snap of his fingers, his way of requesting a cigarette.

Deciding to dismiss Hans, she reached for the mike. She'd grown to love this aspect of the job—feeling people warming towards her, encouraging them to laugh and talk away long journeys, which otherwise might prove tedious. And she liked to stop for a chat in the hotels. It wouldn't be difficult—concentrating on entertaining them, instead of letting Hans provoke her.

Outlining the route they would follow; down the Autostrada to Naples, then forward to Sorrento, she felt him giving her the occasional sideways glance. Again, at their coffee stop, she caught him watching her while she dealt with the inevitable queries.

Suddenly, she couldn't restrain her irritation; outside the coach, she grabbed him by the shirt sleeve: "Something wrong?"

"Just . . . noticing how you cope."

It didn't occur to Joanne that he could be having anything but derogatory thoughts about her methods.

"After all you said!" she exclaimed, forgetting her good intentions. "Can't you give me a break? Get on with your work, and leave me to manage mine! When I can't, I'll ask for help!"

As if she hadn't said enough, she added, "And I'll have to be desperate to turn to you!"

The hand he'd raised to remove hers from his sleeve was suspended, immobile, while she was speaking.

"I don't know who you think you are!" Joanne finished, as their tourists crossed to them. She was confronted by Hans's level gaze. Only now she saw his lips twitch, as if at some amusing secret.

The atmosphere, however, improved. In an effort to be congenial, he chatted occasionally, and kept his eyes on the road. By the time they checked in at their Sorrento hotel, she was congratulating herself on her handling of him and Hans appeared to have accepted her remarks as justified.

Once their clients were installed in their

rooms, and the baggage despatched in the hotel lift, Joanne went to check the coach. She scanned the racks, glanced beneath seats, then collected her possessions. As she retrieved the Company folder, a printed sheet fluttered to the floor. Joanne gasped. Wasn't this the form she ought to have left in Rome for delivery in Berne by the courier on the returning coach? Addressed to their parent company, it reported on the Swiss hotel— new, it had been included only recently in the itinerary. Scowling, Joanne checked her instructions. Yes—the form should have been left behind. She dared not entrust it to the post, so what alternative had she? Maybe she could find another coach returning to Berne . . . But how—except by asking Hans? And that would involve considerable loss of face.

Leaning against her seat, she started when the driver's door opened.

Hans glanced across: "Still here? I didn't see you. It's time you were preparing for dinner. You'll only just make a quick shower . . ."

He retrieved the things for which he'd returned, waiting by the passenger door for her. But he didn't release her hand on assisting her to alight. He was staring hard at

James's ring. He gave a low whistle: "That must be worth something!"

Joanne nodded, shrugged.

"I've said the wrong thing again," he murmured.

"Well, I've told you why I'm here, haven't I?" She tried, and failed, to keep bitterness from her voice: "Maybe if instead, he gave more of his time and concern, I'd be happier. And if he stopped assuming he can buy his way through . . ." She paused. "He's like everybody with money—can't understand real people."

"Real people?"

"Those forced to earn their living—work, like . . ."

". . . coach drivers?" His cold blue eyes were suddenly alive with wicked amusement. Joanne eyed his crumpled shirt, the grubby cravat he had knotted at his neck to check the perspiration which trickled from him. She nodded.

He chuckled, flung a comradely arm about her shoulders as they hurried indoors. "At last, we have a common denominator—the need to earn our bread!"

At the stairs, he stopped, turned to her: "I behaved badly this morning, I was in a foul

mood—unconnected with you, just . . .
another problem. You were wrong afterwards, though, I intended no criticism by
watching you—only interest."

Confused, Joanne went to her room—
acutely aware of his arm across her shoulders.
Whatever else, he was a disturbing man.

While she showered and changed, she tried
phrasing the words asking his aid in ensuring
that wretched form reached its destination.
But inspiration failed to reveal the approach
most likely to win his co-operation.

Lingering after dinner over their wine and
cigarettes (which Hans produced from a remarkably elegant case) Joanne was struggling
still to frame her request. In desperation, she
opened her bag, then tossed the form on to
the table. "You can say 'I told you so' now,
that I was getting too clever—this is where I
climb down and ask your advice."

"Should have been left with the other
courier in Rome, shouldn't it?" Hans said,
after a cursory look. "What will you do?"

"I was hoping you'd suggest something."

"Indeed? I understood I was to leave you to
manage your work." His eyes glinted, but if
he felt like smiling, he had the instinct firmly
controlled.

"I've been honest—admitted I've got myself into a fix."

"And if you were with some driver who refused assistance . . . ?"

"I—I'd find some way out." Joanne wished she were half so confident as she sounded. The form was thrust into her hand.

"Very well."

She felt her teeth sink into her lip and glanced apprehensively, across the table. Hans smiled and stood up.

"Come . . . the bar is almost deserted—let us have a drink, and discuss your problem."

Waiting for Hans, Joanne noticed someone in earnest conversation with a barman. He wore a white suit—she was sure she recognized the man she'd seen that first day at the airport.

As Hans approached with their drinks, she shrugged, dismissing the stranger. She'd often remarked, hadn't she, that one always came across the same people. But this man was watching her.

Hans set a glass before her, occupied the chair opposite; "Well?" His eyes met hers challengingly. "How can I, a mere driver, help you in this difficulty?"

Joanne fidgeted with the form which he'd

returned to her. "Don't you know anyone in Sorrento who's returning to Berne—or even to Rome—with one of our tours?"

With deliberation, Hans extracted the paper from her fingers. "I will see that this reaches its destination."

"You? How? You'll be here in Sorrento."

"I have business in Berne," he appeared amused. "I am flying there the first free day."

"*You?*"

Hans laughed—a long, loud laugh which irritated so much Joanne was tempted to snatch back that form. Only—*if* he spoke the truth, she mustn't aggravate him.

"Impossible, you are thinking—me, a coach driver, having business trips which necessitate flying across Europe!"

"Well, er . . ."

He smiled. "I do not coincide then with your idea of a businessman? Perhaps that is as misconceived as your assumption that people can be categorized according to their financial status?"

"Perhaps . . ." Bewildered again, she was struggling to find some point to this conversation.

"Correct me if I am wrong," Hans

persisted, "but I sense that these dreadful people with money have made you feel . . . how do you say—like a fish without water?"

He was dangerously near the truth. What had started him on this? It was irrelevant to her request for help.

"Well . . . ?" His steady gaze was daring her to evade the question.

Oh, what was it to her if the fellow saw he'd found a tender spot? Joanne nodded.

"I am sorry."

She jerked her eyes to his face. Why should he apologize for a section of the community to which he'd never aspire, much less belong? But his expression was concealed as he studied the document in front of him. He sipped his drink. "Maybe you should not be so hasty, Joanne—lumping people together, judging them—nor filling out forms. See, you should examine always, the small print. You have not signed this . . ."

She looked as his bronzed forefinger indicated the foot of the page, observing that his hands were well-scrubbed, well-manicured. Joanne scribbled her name where appropriate; about to flick over the form, her hand was checked by his.

"Tell me—are you less careless with confidences?"

He seemed to be playing some game tonight—a game without reason. Again, she knew Hans wouldn't let her escape. She sighed. "I can be discreet when necessary. Why?"

He released her hand, turned over the form, inviting her further scrutiny. Beneath the lines of instructions was the address of their parent company in Berne. For the first time Joanne read the owner's name. She looked at it, blinked, looked again.

Hans Lindt.

A hearty laugh filled the bar, a laugh directed at her discomfiture—the laugh of her employer.

2

SHATTERED, Joanne faced the cause of her tumult across the pavement café table. Hans returned her gaze, unblinkingly. He would—he was in a position to trap people into sweeping generalizations about those in authority, about those with money!

How could she have known he wasn't just any old driver?

He was smiling now, infuriatingly, making her feel small—and extremely angry. He'd played a rotten trick, and succeeded, admirably! But *why* had he—why, indeed—taken to driving his own coaches all over Europe?

"It was not only for kicks," Hans began, eventually, her displeasure warranting some explanation; "If you'd known immediately my identity, you would have been more inhibited. And I have to remain incognito; Stella knows me, of course, she is Senior Courier, has been with our subsidiary for years. I was afraid she'd given it away when she introduced us, then I noticed my name meant nothing to you."

31

"But why put me in the picture now?"

"Impulse."

"Because you wanted a laugh—at my expense!"

"No. I had to shake you. I felt insulted by your opinion of those of us who have . . . well, financial security. *I've* never considered money, nor possessions, *that* important!"

"Sorry."

Hans remained silent momentarily, then continued, quietly: "And I wanted you to know the truth, you are . . . different. I'm sick of being *me* only when I fly back to my office."

"Your choice, surely? Why do this, anyway?"

"Is that important? I brought you away from the hotel so we could forget business . . ."

"I'd like to know."

Hans shrugged. "One of my drivers got me mad—accused me of sitting contentedly behind my impressive desk, giving orders, comprehending nothing about conditions on the road."

"So . . . ?"

"I fired him—set out to prove him wrong."

"And?"

"I hate it. But I gave myself until the end of

the season to show . . . that I can take it, I guess. Once I start something I do not give up."

Despite her annoyance, Joanne was warming to him; she smiled. "What's the worst part—dealing with couriers like me?"

Hans shook his head. "No—it conflicts too much with my home life."

Her instinctive response to his honesty froze. It hadn't occurred to her before that he probably had a wife somewhere. Joanne imagined some ultra-smart, jet-set woman—in a fantastic apartment on the outskirts of Berne. She glanced at him.

Yes, he was attractive, all right. She could understand any woman resenting his long absences from home. Well, she'd never increase the problems. She'd had experience in her old job of keeping married men at a distance.

Hans, watching her, seemed . . . puzzled. Joanne forced herself to concentrate on the brightly-lit scene around them, to comment on the crowds thronging the square. But his remarks were becoming monosyllabic. Within half an hour Joanne, excusing herself from the growing awkwardness, returned to the hotel.

She found she couldn't sleep; Hans had shaken her. And she wasn't sure she believed his reasons for taking over as a driver. Nobody would do that—would they? She tried, and failed, to imagine James spending months as a reporter for his father's Fleet Street newspaper. She knew that, however provoked, he'd leave his magnificent office only for a business lunch or prestigious meeting.

She had to admit Hans certainly had something special—and to acknowledge (away from him) that he was . . . likeable.

*　　*　　*

Next morning, Joanne determined to regard Hans as no more than a common-or-garden driver. "A very common one at times," she added to herself, when they'd stopped for coffee and she overheard some of the language he used with other drivers. She recognized, though, that he'd a remarkable knack of getting on with everyone, on equal terms. An assumed ability, perhaps, to make his role convincing?

Feeling his eyes on her, she pretended indifference. But before reaching the coach he'd flung an arm round her shoulders, grinning when this brought an appreciative whistle from his driving colleagues.

"Your demure English ears are not accustomed to such earthy phrases—sorry! I keep forgetting your genteel upbringing."

"It was very ordinary," Joanne retorted, realizing that she enjoyed their verbal battles. "My parents are very advanced, though—for owners of a tiny bookshop near Ripon! They sent me to grammar school, then—eventually—after studying at Evening Classes, I was considered fit to mingle with others!"

Watching Hans pale, she smiled good-naturedly; but before she could put him at ease, he'd spoken; ". . . which you do with becoming grace, I am sure."

Joanne suspected he was teasing, but he confirmed otherwise. "*You* need never let people make you feel inferior."

She was relieved when Mr. and Mrs. Johnson joined them. About her own age, they were always good for a laugh, and made it easier to treat Hans simply as a colleague, which was safer. She'd have to be made of stone to feel no reaction when his arm went about her.

The scenery that day, along the coast road

to Amalfi, took Joanne's breath away. She enthused with the rest over picturesque houses clustering round inlets along the rocky coastline. Then she delighted in helping the four middle-aged schoolmistresses in her party to choose *the* spot for a photograph of Positano.

She found she'd relegated Hans to the back of her consciousness—where he belonged.

Stopping to explore the Emerald Grotto, however, Hans entered into the holiday spirit, drawing her uncomfortably close to his side in the dim cavern. Though this delighted their tourists, it disturbed Joanne. In public she couldn't push him away without appearing unsporting—but how could she cope if he persisted in contriving this proximity?

In Amalfi, after lunching as a group, their holidaymakers were free to explore.

"I hope you swim?" Hans asked her as the others wandered away.

She nodded, she'd every intention of doing so and was wearing a bikini beneath her dress.

The water was a welcome escape from the heat glaring back from white buildings and wide promenade. And her swimming prowess impressed Hans: "I believe at your grammar school you were champion of all aquatic events!"

Joanne grinned, "Well, just a few."

After a quick towelling, Hans tossed himself on to the beach. There seemed little point in not joining him—it was too hot for walking far in an unfamiliar town.

He glanced at his watch which, she'd noticed, he'd not removed before entering the sea.

"Completely waterproof, of course—nothing but the best!" she baited him.

"Certainly—because it is Swiss."

"Because you can pay the price!"

"Don't, Joanne—this spoils you." Hans had rolled over, was regarding her solemnly above tinted glasses.

"What does?"

"Petty remarks against those who happen to be born into families with money. It makes no difference to the people they are."

"No?" She gave him a scathing look, calculated to silence him. It did—most effectively. Collecting his belongings, Hans rose swiftly and strode off. Joanne felt loneliness stab as his figure grew indistinct in the shimmering heat haze.

This was, indisputably, her fault. Joanne

sighed, turned over, burying her head in her arms. Now the sun scorched the nape of her neck; she'd suffer afterwards if she lingered here for long.

She settled for a stroll along the promenade. After only a few metres she sensed she was being followed. She swung round, eyes raking the crowds, expecting, hoping, to see Hans . . . He might have decided to hang around, in case she tried to find him.

Disappointed that she couldn't see anyone resembling him, Joanne crossed the broad thoroughfare. The sensation of being followed persisted; despite the heat, a shiver ran up her spine. She tried telling herself the bikini, damp still beneath her dress, had caused the sudden chill—and knew it hadn't.

Passing seafront hotels and shops, she realized she must discover if somebody was tailing her and, feigning interest in a shop window protruding on to the pavement, used it as a mirror. About twenty paces behind her, someone else stopped. A man—wearing a white safari suit. Was it coincidence? The garb was common enough out here—yet she was certain this was the man who'd been watching her at the airport and in the hotel bar. Her heart pounding, Joanne walked on then turned suddenly into the warren of streets close to the cathedral.

This time glass covering a framed street plan gave her a rear-view.

She saw the white-suited man come round the corner then dart into an alley as though startled to find her waiting.

She was trembling now—she must find somewhere to hide: the cathedral looked the most likely place. She started running up the seemingly endless steps to its door and developed a near-unbearable stitch but she dared not rest—nor look back. Reaching the door at last, she slipped her towel across bare arms, and scuttered inside.

Panting, legs aching, Joanne glanced longingly towards the seats. But she must get away from that door—mingle with the sightseers. Unfortunately, few people were looking round and her yellow dress was much too conspicuous. Then her alert ears identified a door closing. Someone had entered. Her scalp prickled, cautioning her not to look round—but she had to know . . .

The gleam of white was unmistakable in the gloomy interior. Her view was uninterrupted, therefore he'd have spotted *her*. She'd have to get away. Thankful that her sandals made no sound, she dashed through a group of soft-footed nuns. But she could hear other footsteps—firm, swift, ringing on the ground as they approached.

The magnificent building became menacing—a prison. Panic had driven her to the worst possible place. Outdoors, she'd been safe—amongst the many visitors. She must escape . . . She almost sobbed with relief when she noticed the door in the far wall of a side chapel. Running across, she began wrestling with its iron handle. Those footsteps were gaining on her now . . .

The door swung open admitting bright sunlight and warm, heavy air, and emerging, Joanne checked her instinct to race towards the street below. Hiding behind an angle of the wall, she waited.

The man in the white suit came out. Now she knew he'd shadowed her. And this *was* the man she'd seen previously.

What was he after?

No time now to consider that—she must watch him, be sure where he was. She'd lose the slender advantage of having him in front if she didn't concentrate. A few steps down, he paused, looked to left and right and glanced back. Joanne dropped behind a rotund priest and, risking another look, saw the man turn away, frowning. He gave a barely perceptible shrug and then started two at a time down the remaining steps.

Gulping in air, trying to steady her rocky knees, she stood on the steps wondering what to do next. Satisfied now that he couldn't pounce on her from behind, should she let him go . . . ?

Cautiously, Joanne followed, eyes riveted on this pursuer turned pursued. Reaching the junction with the promenade, he looked uncertainly about. As she gained on him, Joanne saw him repeat the shrug and realized he thought he'd lost her. She withdrew, gladly, from the hide-and-seek, her thudding heart-beat gradually steadying.

She was thirsty and needed to find a café—if time allowed.

The public clock, in an ornamental tower, showed almost three o'clock. Her frightening experience had lasted only a fraction of the time she'd supposed. How easily she'd been scared beyond all reckoning.

Relieved that she needn't rush in the afternoon sun, Joanne permitted herself to peer into the quaint shops she passed, smiling at the local women on upright chairs in open doorways.

Eventually finding a café, she glanced nervously about for the white-suited man, then chose a table in the shade. The café was crowded, its waitresses slow, but Joanne had ceased to care. She was sitting, at last; after a quiet drink she'd return to the coach, to the protection of her tourists—and Hans. No matter that they had rowed, he'd be at her side—solid, dependable, reassuring.

Joanne lingered over the iced drink, half-dozing in the relief following that hair-raising chase. With a start, she realized it must be time she headed for the coach. She glanced, over her shoulder, towards that same clock.

It couldn't be . . . ! A little before three—that was the time previously. No! Don't say the thing had stopped. She watched its gilded hands, willing them to move. They were motionless.

She gulped down the remains of her drink, beckoned the waitress and fumbled for cash to pay the bill.

The hand smacked down on her shoulder, stinging the bare, sun-burned flesh, bringing tears to her eyes.

"What the hell are you doing?"

Hans.

He picked up her bill, tossed coins from his pocket on to the table and—keeping a hand firm on Joanne's shoulder—steered her away. He forced her, running, along the promenade.

"I'm sorry," she began, but he interrupted, fiercely, "Save that—reserve your breath for hurrying. We've an hour less for the return journey—pray we don't encounter traffic!"

"I suppose they're all waiting in the coach?"

"You suppose correctly!" Hans jerked her onwards, sliding his hand down her arm to grip more surely. She could feel each unrelenting finger. If she'd considered him curt, that was mild compared with his fury.

"Whatever shall I say to them?"

"Nothing. Leave everything to me—it'll be less devastating than anything you might concoct."

Crossing to their vehicle, Hans moved his hand to her elbow, his other arm supporting her. As Joanne struggled to free herself he sighed, "This is no time for conflicting opinions," and added, in German, as they reached the steps, "Follow my lead."

He assisted her, quite unnecessarily, into

the coach and turned, smilingly, to say, "You must forgive the delay. Joanne was overcome by heat. Fortunately, I found her at the café where she was recovering."

A sympathetic murmur rose behind Joanne, making her feel *the* fraud of all time. Why had Hans lied to cover for her? Contemplating the concerned questioning that would come her way, she wondered how she'd respond.

Hans soon had the coach mobile but his mouth was set, grimly. All the way along the snaking cliff road he drove swiftly. Joanne marvelled at his skill. Who would have suspected he hadn't spent all his working life handling huge vehicles?

He made up half an hour *en route*, enabling their clients to freshen up before dinner. Joanne saw him smile to himself.

As the tourists disappeared into the hotel—with Joanne's assurance that she had recovered—she glanced anxiously towards Hans. He collected together his possessions and reached for the door handle.

"I am sorry, you know," she started, "I haven't a watch and . . ."

"That's obvious," he interrupted, jumping down on to the road.

"I'm trying to apologize—and to thank you for making my excuses."

His eyes met hers across the driving seat. She noticed perspiration trickling down his face from fair hair clinging damply in strands. And she *was* sorry—for her carelessness, for vexing him, for forcing a furious drive in this heat.

Hans sighed, wearily, "Look, I need a shower—desperately. Don't want to give this another thought till I've eaten. We'll have this out, privately, afterwards."

They ate in awkward silence. Joanne itched to mention her disappearance and be done with the matter, but those hard, blue eyes demanded acquiescence.

"Come . . ." Hans commanded when, dinner at last over, their tourists had departed. In the lift he was silent, pre-occupied. Joanne weighed her chances. Was this enough to make him sack her? *Could* he sack her?—she was employed by the sub-sidiary company. Doubtless, if sufficiently provoked, Hans could engineer her dismissal.

If that happened, what on earth would she do? Not return to London so soon—to James—to admit she'd failed.

Hans closed the door of his room, quietly,

and pointed to a chair. Joanne chose to stand. It'd be easier to take his reprimand—to dash from the room when she was dismissed.

He walked to the window, stood, back turned—thinking, or so it seemed—then swung round to face her. "You will never do that again! You kept everyone waiting and . . . and I didn't know where the blazes to look for you."

"I'm sor . . ." Joanne began. Hans nodded.

"*Sorry*. You said. But that doesn't compensate for my . . . anxiety."

"Anxiety?"

He lowered his eyelids, as though to conceal something. ". . . er . . . my couriers are my responsibility. I can't let them disappear . . . abandon them in some strange town—much as I might feel so inclined!"

Despite his tone, Joanne sensed already that Hans wouldn't fire her. More, she realized he'd been genuinely concerned for her safety. Relieved and surprised, she couldn't stop her lips twitching. "Am I reprieved?" she asked, mischievously, before she could bite back the words.

"Don't interrupt. I haven't nearly finished with you! You've let the Company down, our clients—and made me drive like a . . . like a maniac!"

"No," she protested; "you drove with skill, and confidence in your ability." She felt her colour rising as Hans, eyebrows arching, scrutinized her.

He shrugged, turned again to the window. Against the night sky, the glass reflected back his grin. "I suppose I shouldn't have stormed off, leaving you . . ."

"You were provoked."

"*Ja!*" He ran a hand through his hair. "I was provoked." Fresh from the shower, his hair was soft, lightened by the day's sun. When he faced her, Joanne noticed he looked younger; for once, vulnerable. "You, young woman," he declared, advancing, "have it in you to ruin years of hard work—and get away with it!"

"I don't understand." And nor did she.

Hans seized her shoulders, propelling her towards the full-length mirror: "Take a look—at those enormous brown, innocent eyes—at that delectably feminine figure—then tell me you don't use all that to defeat every man—to defeat me!"

"I've never consciously done that."

She felt Hans sigh against her, his hands

47

were biting into her shoulders. "No, I don't believe you have. And there's the danger."

Intending now to challenge him, Joanne glanced up. He was gnawing his lip. He turned her to face him. "If—if it were conscious, I'd insist that you . . . turn it off, or something. As it is . . ." Again, he gave that tiny shrug. "Only remember—I'll tolerate no nonsense that might jeopardize my Company."

"It wasn't nonsense . . ." Joanne stopped. If she mentioned being followed it'd only sound like an excuse. "I . . . hadn't the right time."

"I know," Hans said, a shade curtly. "We'll rectify that. Meanwhile . . ."

". . . try a bit harder?"

He nodded, a smile enhancing his beautifully etched lips. "Now you can buy me a drink—don't forget you are indebted for your lemonade or whatever!"

"I had forgotten." Her embarrassment increased with his laugh. And still Hans held her—close, very close, to him.

"I also owe you thanks, for neatly retrieving the situation."

"Forget it. It wasn't to save your face, I'll do anything to preserve our clients' goodwill." His sharp tone was belied by the way he was holding her, his eyes seeking her own, his fingers suddenly caressing her bare arms.

Hands clasped before her, Joanne started her habitual fiddling with her ring.

Hans looked down and abruptly released her. "Let's get that drink," he suggested, coldly.

*   *   *

Next morning Hans was absent from the breakfast table. He had left a message that he'd be away two days while their tourists, at leisure in Sorrento, wouldn't require the coach.

Once he had gone, Joanne felt uneasy lest something should go wrong; and yet he must feel certain she could cope or he would not have left. And she missed him.

She missed those blue eyes meeting hers—challenging though they often were. She missed their mealtime conversation, which was becoming amiable . . . and chance encounters on the stairs, in the lounge or bar. She missed, too, sharing the secret of his identity.

Joanne told herself this was ridiculous; Hans was still the man she'd disliked when they were introduced, who often showed scant patience.

Yet there had been moments when he'd changed, swiftly. When their eyes had held in something akin to . . . comradeship. Moments, too, when his eyes had prophesied lips coming down, hard, on hers. Only—as last evening—those lips had come no nearer. And she'd been disappointed. For the first time since becoming engaged, Joanne wondered if she'd refused even to look at another man because James would fall short if she made comparisons. And so now there was Hans, and she was compelled to admit she'd wanted to respond when something in his expression revealed his need, unreservedly.

Remember, she cautioned herself, he has domestic problems—which, even now, he may be resolving. With his wife?

Despite all misgivings, Joanne was glad when their dinner table was again set for two. She was into her main course before, looking up, she gasped as Hans slid on to his chair. He was wearing an exquisitely-cut dove grey suit, perfectly complemented by lilac tie and shirt.

"You look very grand!" she exclaimed without thinking, and Hans frowned warningly. "I'm trying to remain inconspicuous—came straight from the office. Carry on eating—you haven't seen the eighth wonder of the world. Even I have more than one outfit."

Joanne stifled her laugh as Hans presented his on-duty smile to the waiter.

"Good trip?" she enquired, trying to sound disinterested.

Hans started scowling, checked that and nodded: "Business-wise, satisfactory," he responded, precluding further questions. What did this mean—that his domestic scene was upsetting still? Allowing her no chance to work things out, Hans retrieved an envelope from his pocket.

"Receipt for that form I handled on your behalf. The boss has overlooked your negligence—*this time*!"

Joanne smiled across: "Thank you very much."

Hans gave that familiar small shrug—something else, Joanne discovered, which she had missed.

"Careful," he cautioned, as she reached for

the envelope, "and don't express surprise—not in here."

Mystified, she allowed one hand to explore the package, but she remained bewildered. She glanced curiously at Hans, who beamed suddenly, and nodded.

Joanne opened the envelope on her lap, gazing disbelievingly at a neat, gold, urgently-ticking watch.

"Not one word," he warned, beneath his breath, "not yet . . ."

"But . . ."

"Later. Eat your dinner."

Immediately afterwards they left, clients in tow, for a night-club. Joanne suspected Hans of enjoying the delayed explanation. In place round her wrist, the watch drew her eyes, frequently—under Hans's amused observation.

Only after the coach had emptied at the hotel was there a chance for the private word for which she'd longed.

"What a reward!" Hans exclaimed. "Watching your astonishment—then later, the smile you couldn't quite restrain whenever you checked the time!"

"But why, Hans—why give me this?"

"So you do not wreck my Company's schedules."

"Do you provide all couriers with watches?"

"Only the ones against whom I must safeguard myself. Those threatening the equilibrium of . . . things."

Light flooding from the hotel revealed his grin—boyish, totally unsuitable for the Managing Director of a Company whose many coaches toured every continental country.

"Don't dare remove that from your wrist," he continued, with a severity of tone quite unconnected with his laughing eyes; "it is waterproof—and *almost* as good as mine. You've no excuse for not wearing the thing!"

"I don't know how to thank you!" Joanne exclaimed.

"No?" Hans demanded—and chuckled. Still in his seat behind the wheel, the night air coming through the open window was stirring his hair. Sitting only a little way away, Joanne clenched her hands against the instinct to reach out and . . . touch . . . to trace with caressing fingers the line of that sun-tanned cheek. Hans was inviting her to be incautious, to forget James; to forget . . . whatever situation he had left at home.

Perhaps *because* they both had problems she couldn't hold back completely.

And just to thank him—that couldn't hurt. She leaned across, brushed his cheeks with her lips.

"Thank you, Hans."

He caught her to him, awkwardly, because of their positioning, but his lips found hers surely. Pulses awakened instantly, throbbing with the attraction she could ignore no longer. She moved, about to slide a hand to his nape. The diamond on her third finger sparkled.

Hans sighed, drew away. "*Ja*," he muttered, nodding to himself. All boyishness evaporated, he looked, and sounded, weary. "Better go in," he continued, ruefully. "Almost, I suggested the back seat is more comfortable—and more private."

She ought to feel relieved that he wasn't suggesting any such thing. Yet she felt only an aching emptiness. Hans opened the door, sprang out, locked up. Feet crunched on the tarmac as he came round the coach.

Deep inside her, intuition insisted that Hans needed her—outrageous though that might seem. Not as a girl to embrace on a

darkened night, maybe—as someone to . . .
listen.

So much about Hans bewildered her; why
was he here instead of in his office? Why did
he frequently stare into space as if wrestling
with some insuperable problem? Was there
trouble within the Company, or was the
cause more personal? Either way, she wanted
only to understand, would give anything to
have him confide in her. But how could she
encourage that?

Hans beckoned from the passenger door,
"Coming . . . ?" He seemed drained, tense,
depressed.

She had to try. "What is it, Hans?"

Surprised, he looked up at her, tried to iron
out his frown but failed.

"And don't just shrug," Joanne persisted.

He came back into the coach, smiled and
shook his head. "You know too many of my
secrets!"

"Oh." Why be hurt, why feel he'd
slammed a door on her? It shouldn't matter
what Hans said, or did, to her.

"And I know too much about you," he
murmured, beside her seat now, raising her
hand, inspecting her ring again, "to steal
kisses."

"That was given," she whispered and felt the hand on hers tighten. He pulled her to her feet: "Come on, woman—I've been up since six. I'm flat out—nearly asleep on my feet."

Joanne had to smile, "You convinced me you were awake just now!" She noticed his eyes were laughing.

Closing up and locking the coach, Hans motioned her to wait.

He drew her into the shadow of the vehicle, held her so close Joanne felt his heart hammering against her. "I cannot tell you what is wrong," he confessed, at last, in German, "cannot find the words. But . . . thank you for asking." He gave her a hug and released her. She heard him whistling, tunelessly, without joy, as he followed a few paces behind her through the foyer.

At breakfast next morning, Hans seemed composed. Once they'd set out with their tourists towards Pompeii, she found his patience thin. Too often, his fingers flicked, requesting a cigarette.

Arrived at their destination and the coach empty, he snapped, "See you at three sharp," and turned on his heel.

"But, Hans . . ." Joanne protested, catching up with him.

"Well?"

"I haven't been here before and . . ."

"There's an English-speaking guide! Surely you can manage to trail round in his wake?" With that he spun round and strode off towards a café beside the cameo factory.

Joanne stared after him, wondering if she'd imagined their brief spell of empathy last night.

Hurrying to catch up with the quartet of schoolmistresses who were waiting for her, Joanne reminded herself it wasn't *Hans* who should be arousing her longings for any kind of sharing. But she'd never felt this concerned about anyone. James had always seemed self-sufficient. She'd adored him at first and he'd basked in her admiration, until he began to take her for granted. She wished suddenly for some sign that James needed her.

*   *   *

James's letter arrived next morning, astonishing her. He'd tired already of their unsatisfactory relationship. He was flying out to Rome, where their coach stopped on the return journey, and he'd reserved a room at their hotel.

"Better news, I see . . ." Hans remarked as she folded the letter.

"James arrives in Rome when we do."

His enigmatic blue eyes revealed nothing, and his smooth voice conveyed no reaction. "You have soon brought him to heel!"

He made no further comment until they were leaving Sorrento. Checking off baggage with her, he cleared his throat—if it had been anyone else she'd have thought him anxious. "I trust that, whatever the outcome of your reunion, you'll remain with the Company for the rest of the season . . ."

"You don't think much of me, do you, Hans! You're not the only one who stays the course once they start something."

Hans straightened his back and grinned. "Good."

Joanne realized suddenly that he was pleased she'd asserted herself. As she started helping people to board the coach, she wondered if Hans had observed and understood how James had drained spirit, as well as self-confidence, from her.

3

JOANNE began to think they'd never reach Rome.

A lorry had shed its load of melons across the Autostrada, causing several minor accidents, and an unbelievable delay.

When, eventually, they booked into the hotel, Reception told her James had telephoned, twice, from the airport. He had since arrived, by cab.

She was upset—she'd intended meeting his flight. She had the evening free and was longing to know why he'd come. She had to contain her impatience, through allocating rooms, sorting suitcases and settling her tourists into the dining-room.

And the hotel hadn't helped—they'd complicated matters by assigning them a different dining-room area from their previous visit.

Three times, she'd had to retrieve clients who had somehow got past her table where, sticky, hot and edgy, she was trying to sort the chaos. And Hans had disappeared so she'd no assistance from him.

He flopped on to his chair as she started her lasagne. Her eyes must have asked where he'd been, though she did not voice curiosity.

"Had to make an urgent phone call," he explained, frowning.

"Not depressing news, I hope?"

Hans hesitated and she recognized his longing to confide but he shook his head. "Leave it—you're in a hurry to get out tonight."

Rebuffed, Joanne looked away, hastily. She noticed James then, across the room. He was watching her and appeared to have been doing so for some time. Aware of her gaze, he rose and ambled towards their table, greeting her unsmilingly. Joanne introduced the two men. She felt Hans assessing James and wished he'd mind his own business.

James was scowling. "Thought you'd be here earlier."

"We were delayed."

"Fine welcome I get—coming all this way, after weeks. You might, at least, have been there."

Joanne swallowed, hard. This was dreadful.

"Joanne is working," Hans remarked, his eyes glacial, earning her profound gratitude.

"Working most efficiently," he added, smiling at her.

James snorted, "She needn't work, she knows that."

"Perhaps Joanne prefers to work . . ." Hans suggested.

Given time to recover, she tried to smooth over the growing friction: "Have you finished dinner, James—why not join us?"

"This table isn't very large," Hans said, quietly. "Shall I move?"

"Of course not."

"You come over to me, Joanne." James didn't make it a question: "I've plenty to say and can't stay as long as I had intended."

Instead of acquiescing, as once she would, Joanne was irritated by James's assumption that she'd drop everything for him. She glanced for guidance to Hans and observed his astonishment at her hesitation. He spread his hands expansively. "You've ensured our clients are content, what you do next is, I would think, up to you."

She felt James's eyes boring into the top of her head, willing her assent and remembered how he'd taken her for granted. She'd come away to prove she wasn't some . . . chattel to be discarded then retrieved at will. "I'll stay where I am, it'll confuse the waiters if I swop tables mid-meal."

"I see." James strode off.

Hans was watching her. He looked pleased. She wanted to make him share her uneasiness.

"You could have agreed to him joining us."

"I could," Hans concurred, his face a mask again. "I could have done, or said, all manner of things . . ."

Abashed, Joanne recalled the words Hans had found for her to answer James. She smiled at him.

"But you did speak up for me—thanks."

Hans nodded acknowledgement and continued eating, smiling slightly.

★   ★   ★

The meal over, James claimed her immediately; with a curt "Good night" to Hans, he led her away. Joanne felt suddenly lost; alone with this stranger who was supposed to be her fiancé, in this city far from home.

"Didn't hire a car," he informed her,

"have to fly back tomorrow—it's not worth-while. Where shall we go? Suggest some-where, and I'll call a cab."

"I don't know where to suggest."

"Thought that was your job—knowing places of interest?"

"All right then, the Colosseum, it's floodlit after dark, it's ever so . . ."

"Oh, not there, *please*! It'll be overrun by tourists."

"So what? They're just ordinary people like us."

"Like . . . ? Heaven forbid! Joanne, what has become of you?"

"Well, I'm not a snob . . ."

Briefly, James seemed embarrassed. "Sorry, Joanne, but I hate seeing you working with these people."

"The job's fascinating. They're a friendly crowd, and I enjoy helping . . . well, to make the tour succeed. I love being involved, one of a team."

"Some team—if that driver's a sample of the talent!"

"If only you knew!" Joanne thought, and stifled the urge to reveal Hans's identity.

★   ★   ★

The evening wasn't the success she'd hoped. The Eternal City's splendours were lost on James, who was capable only of criticism. As the throngs thinned out and he ceased complaining of crowded streets, he declared Rome . . . dead. Unimpressed by the Forum, the Palatine Hill, the Tiber, he hastened her back to the hotel.

By this time Joanne was containing the impulse to remind James this visit was his idea. If she annoyed him, she'd never learn why he'd come.

Strolling in the hotel garden, he began, "I've been wondering—about us. Maybe you were right, giving us a break."

What was he going to say? That he'd realized he needed her? A month ago the prospect would have elated her, now . . . She wasn't sure. Tonight she'd seen James differently, knew now that she needed time—a great deal of time—before committing herself.

James went to the garden-swing and patted the cushion beside him. He placed an arm round her, set the swing in motion and buried his face in her neck. Through the glass doors she noticed Hans, alone, in the bar. She wished James would be quick in coming to the point, because she was thirsty and had just decided she'd insist they go in.

His lips claiming hers were hard, demanding, reminding Joanne of the ecstasy they'd once shared. Her body began to respond. She'd forgotten how, infuriating though he might be, this close James was complete excitement. For several minutes her senses dispelled thought in desire—until she noticed something missing. She'd become detached from sensation, an observer, looking for . . . ? What—concern, caring?

"As I said," James continued, between kisses, "the break has been good for us. Back home we were too . . . hemmed in, by circumstances. Restricted . . ."

"You weren't! You went off, time and again, leaving me with your parents."

"Don't you see—they were the reason. Cramping our style. Here, like this, we can give ourselves a fair trial."

"Trial?"

"Why do you think I've come? Out here's ideal—the perfect set-up."

"For what?"

"You can't be that naïve! You're the girl who wears my ring, you surely don't think I'd make the relationship more permanent till we're sure it'd be . . . all right."

Joanne didn't answer. She felt the dull ache of disappointment. Accepted, James aroused her, he always had—but she knew she . . . wouldn't. Not like this, as though she were going in for some kind of exam!

"I'm afraid I don't agree, James—never have agreed, that sex tests whether a marriage will work. It's more than going to bed together."

"It's important, nevertheless."

"Maybe. But then I've never doubted that aspect would be more than all right."

"Then where's the harm in reassuring me?"

Still she hesitated.

"It's what an engagement's for . . ."

He sounded petulant now, and she wondered if she was seeing this side of him for the first time, because before she'd never opposed him. Well, she wouldn't be coerced into something this important.

He snatched at her hand. "You shouldn't have accepted this, if you weren't prepared..."

He got no further; Joanne wrenched herself away from him. Removing his ring from her finger, she thrust it at him. "Have it back then!" she retorted, then dashed in through the bar, head down to conceal her distress.

*　　*　　*

At breakfast next morning Hans seemed pensive but Joanne didn't care—she cared about nothing. The night had been long, and sleepless.

She thought she'd been right, following her instinct. But she had been hasty. James had been the centre of her universe for years. There'd be an enormous gap in her life without him. Maybe they could remain friends, keep in touch . . . If she went with him to the airport, made him see she needed time . . .

She'd always loved James . . . she couldn't be this wrong about him, could she? Last night had been disastrous, but not irrevocable.

The table he'd occupied last evening was vacant. Had he left already? She'd have to write . . .

Hans's blue glance went to the doorway, behind her. It was James.

He came straight across, kissed her as though nothing had occurred. "Come and see me off—I fly at eleven . . ."

She'd been right. It wasn't ended.

"We're going to the Catacombs," Hans protested.

Joanne glared at him. "You don't need me there."

"Of course. It is your job . . ."

"Just a minute," Joanne turned to James. "Wait in the corridor, will you?"

She scowled at Hans, "You know there's a guide at the Catacombs, that we shan't even go inside. No one will miss me." She raised brimming eyes to his. "Please, Hans, this is important."

He sighed, "See him off, if you must—if that's what you really want. Go, by all means, and by Saturday I'll have your replacement out here!"

*　　*　　*

Joanne couldn't bring herself to address Hans until they were alone in the coach, at the Catacombs.

Of course she'd gone there—meekly (to her disgust), unable to ignore what she'd been certain was no idle threat. She determined, nevertheless, that Hans should learn she wasn't obeying him unquestioningly.

"Do you mind telling me why you took it upon yourself to insist I sit around here?" she demanded.

Half-turning in his seat, Hans looked at her. "Are you sure you want to know?"

"It can't be that you consider me irreplaceable—not when you've found fault so often?"

Hans nodded, looked away. "True . . ."

"Why then?"

He waited a moment, then began: "Last night, when you'd gone upstairs, your boy-friend came into the bar. He avoided me, but I couldn't help overhearing . . ." Hans hesitated, then sighed. "If you can, *Liebchen*, forget him."

"What the hell's it to do with you!" Joanne flared, then his expression checked her.

"Tell me the worst . . ."

"You won't like it."

"Today, I don't like anything."

"He was celebrating, he said. He'd discovered you are a puritan—just in time."

"So I am—so what?"

"Listen, Joanne—I don't know about your country, but in mine a gentleman doesn't discuss the woman in his life—least of all in that way."

She breathed deeply, praying the tears she'd restrained so far wouldn't reveal her vulnerability.

"He also," Hans was continuing, then he stopped.

"Go on."

"No, you will be hurt."

"I am already." It was no good pretending, any second her voice would give her away.

"He has someone else lined up."

"All right, Hans, I've got the message." Joanne placed her hands on either side of her head, to still its throbbing—and hide her eyes.

Five minutes ticked laboriously by. Hans remained silent, and—this far—she'd checked the tears. She remembered something.

"That was the reason you forbade my going to the airport, wasn't it?"

"No. It was your duty to come here."

"Come off it! You suspected James wanted the satisfaction of keeping me in tow as well."

Joanne stole a glance at the young man in the driver's seat. Sensing her gaze, Hans turned. "He's not worth losing your pride, Joanne. He . . . well, I can see how he'd make you feel . . . all the things you told me that time. Let him go . . ." Hans reached out, squeezed her hand. "Do not make this the end of the world. Today, you are miserable; soon, little lady, have some fun—and happiness."

He jumped down on to the road, left the coach, giving her a respite, for which she was grateful. His understanding had surprised her. His straightforward appraisal of James, nevertheless, had been a knife thrust.

Minutes later Hans returned with ice-cream, purchased nearby. "Here—eat that. And cheer up, the others will be back all too soon."

*　　*　　*

By evening Joanne was recovering. She dressed carefully for dinner, determined to appear unperturbed by the outcome of James's visit. Hans complimented her on her appearance, conversed pleasantly throughout the meal, then when she rose sprang to his feet.

"What are you doing this evening?"

Astonished, she shrugged. "Having an early night."

"What a waste—you have taken trouble over your face and hair, chosen a becoming dress. You should, how do you say it, hit the town."

Joanne found herself smiling, and couldn't resist asking, "Alone?"

"For what do you take me? I am offering my services as escort—if you could bear that . . ."

"You don't have to be kind!" Instantly, she regretted her words but Hans grinned, though he seemed wary. "There is another approach—*I* need a change, Joanne; will you accompany me—please?"

She smiled. "All right then—thanks."

"Good. Give me ten minutes—I must wear something presentable."

When he rejoined her, Joanne stifled an instinctive exclamation. His light-weight suit was exquisite, his grooming immaculate. Again he was very much the man-about-town.

She realized suddenly that withholding her approval was churlish. "I'm flattered," she remarked, her eyes endorsing her appreciation.

Hans grinned again, giving a mischievous wink. "Let's make this an occasion . . ."

The night-club they visited was unquestionably one of *the* night-spots. Joanne noticed how the barman greeted Hans with deference—noticed, too, that Hans showed neither surprise nor satisfaction. And already she was making comparisons . . . if she'd come here with James . . .

"Joanne," Hans began, "I did not bring you out to have you brooding. Come—we will dance."

Going into his arms, she chuckled, "You needn't worry—you were coming off pretty well!"

"M'm?" He'd either failed to comprehend—or wished her to believe so.

"It's delightful being with someone who doesn't make me feel uncomfortable."

She observed his raised eyebrow, but he said nothing, and she concentrated on dancing. Hans, she learned, was expert, her only regret that he held her so . . . formally. He'd been so understanding today that this seemed incongruous. Soon, worrying what prevented him drawing her close, Joanne stumbled.

Hans immediately pulled her against him, his arm about her tightening. "Or do you object?"

"Of course not."

Before long she relaxed completely, Hans's

chin was against her hair and she knew only the joy of being well-partnered. Contentedly, she let his body direct hers in every step, feeling that she'd found a haven.

Pausing only for the occasional drink, they danced until after midnight, then Joanne sighed: "We've a demanding day tomorrow, Hans, haven't we?"

"I was thinking we ought to leave—though reluctantly, I've enjoyed every minute."

"So have I!"

Hans regarded her quizzically.

Joanne nodded. "Truthfully. With a partner like you, how could I do otherwise!"

He gave a small, acknowledging bow. "I am so pleased all those dreary ballroom lessons in my teens were to some avail!" Then he laughed, offering her his arm as they left.

Inside their taxi, they sat apart, as though they'd lost the intimacy acquired that day. Crossing the hotel foyer, Hans made as if to hurry away. Joanne couldn't let him walk off without showing she appreciated his kindness, his concern, throughout.

"Hans," she began, touching his arm. "You've got me through today, made me see sense—made me happier than I believed possible."

He was staring at her, disbelieving humility in his eyes increasing the affection she felt for him now.

She chuckled, "I've surprised you! Has nobody ever said you're good company?"

"*You* haven't!" He was looking over her head towards the deserted lounge. "Well, Joanne . . ."

"M'm?"

"It is less public in there."

As the lounge door closed, Joanne found she'd no wish to demur. Was it just over twenty-four hours since she'd returned her ring to James? Had she felt so little for him that already she had dismissed him?

Hans led her to a cushioned seat; sitting, he drew her to him. Then he hesitated.

"What's wrong?" she asked.

He shrugged, sighed. "It is not done, is it— the boss making passes. It makes it, for you, difficult to refuse."

Joanne smiled. "We could pretend you're just my driver!"

She felt Hans laugh before kissing her, thoroughly.

On the edge of consciousness memory

niggled—a memory connected with Hans, something threatening this nearness. Joanne banished the thought.

"Tell me more about yourself," he prompted presently. "You were an interpreter, weren't you? Did you train for that on leaving school?"

"Yes."

"And you lived with your parents?"

"No—in London. There's no scope for the job back home."

*　　*　　*

When a distant clock, chiming one, brought her back to the present, Joanne smiled, ruefully. "I did say we've a demanding day ahead . . ."

Walking beside Hans to the door, Joanne felt an irrational sadness as though something inordinately precious was being taken from her. She wanted the reassurance of his arms about her again.

Reaching for the door handle, Hans hesitated. "If—as you claim—you have enjoyed the evening, maybe we could repeat the experiment?"

Joanne didn't reply immediately and Hans

turned to her, his eyes questioning, uncertain.

"I'd love that," she responded, at last.

He caught her to him and his mouth came down hard on hers. Joanne returned his kisses, fiercely.

But later, alone in her room, the memory she'd dismissed returned to plague her. They had been sitting at a pavement café; after Hans had revealed who he was, she had teased him about taking to the road. "What's the worst part—dealing with couriers like me?" she'd asked.

"No—it conflicts too much with my home life."

His home—*who* awaited him there?

During yet another restless night, Joanne realized that she hadn't responded to Hans merely because he was on the spot. She'd been happy with him—happy, also, to admit that her first impression had been entirely wrong.

His sudden flashes of humour proved he wasn't normally either morose or sharp-tongued. And she often caught herself trying to make him laugh, to . . . relax? But he seemed so wary, living on his nerves—because of some worry, perhaps, which explained and excused his mercurial behaviour. Her sympathy aroused, she wanted to understand. While he'd shown concern for her distress, she'd longed increasingly to express *her* concern for his difficulties. Yet if Hans was married and that was going wrong, he must resolve the matter without her aid. She'd never even question him. And she'd be wise to discourage evenings similar to this one which had meant so much. Without knowing more about Hans, she wouldn't risk deeper involvement.

While dressing next morning, Joanne found a new perspective. Hans had offered friendship—*that* she could reciprocate, safely. And she had enough to occupy her. Since beginning the tour, she'd discovered she loved working with people, enjoyed the responsibility synonymous with the job. Stimulating, it used her facility with languages, fulfilled her urge to travel.

Her own smile surprised her as she hurried to the dining-room. "Good morning," she greeted Hans: "I feel infinitely better than this time yesterday—thanks to you."

He glanced up from the roll he was crumbling, aimlessly. He didn't respond, nor attempt a smile.

When the waiter had brought her coffee, Joanne tried again: "I can recommend your treatment for the blues—you proved a true friend."

Still, he remained silent. Torn between the resolution not to pry and her instinct to help, she dismissed her overnight caution.

"Perhaps it's time I shared your problems . . . ?"

Briefly, their eyes met. She noticed how sad Hans looked; but he only shrugged.

"Maybe—some time. *If* you want to listen. Now, however, I am trying to concentrate solely on my job."

Again, Joanne felt rebuffed. This must have been apparent.

"Sorry—I didn't mean to switch off communication so abruptly. Please understand I must ensure our safe arrival in Florence. I cannot permit distractions."

So—she'd learned nothing. Except that her emotions last night weren't dependent solely upon the enchanting music and dancing with Hans, but the culmination of a many-faceted need increasing daily since their introduction.

Once behind the wheel, Hans permitted nothing to diminish his skill. Joanne watched him, covertly, admiring his control. Somehow, from somewhere, she must find comparable self-discipline. It seemed already that her break with James was no more than a welcome release, leaving her free. And what she must do, constantly, was to remind herself that Hans was his own man.

As they settled down for the journey, Joanne realized that from the week-end on, she would have a new driver as well as different tourists. Soon she would remember this fortnight as merely an interlude, and her relationship with Hans as a passing acquaintanceship.

Soon after stopping for coffee on the Autostrada, Henry, one of the passengers, came down the coach from the rear. "There's something wrong with the bus, I'm afraid," he began very quietly.

When Joanne investigated, she found pungent evidence of burning rubber. The windows were open wide, and the fumes wafted towards her. Hastily, she made her way forward to report to Hans. Within moments, he'd drawn off the carriageway and leapt down on to the road. He was frowning, feeling the rear wheel then shaking his hand as though it were hot.

"Well?" Joanne asked.

"It should see us to the next service station."

"And if it doesn't? Hans, if it's one of the tyres, can't you change it?"

"It is not a tyre."

"Then what? Is it safe to go on?"

"Of course," he replied, too quickly. "Besides, it is only a few metres to a garage. Now get back in the coach, Joanne—tell everyone all will be well. But we shall stop at the garage, for a minor adjustment."

"Is it only minor?"

"That is what you will tell them."

"If you say so," she acquiesced, annoyed because he hadn't confided in her.

Before she boarded the coach, Hans seized her arm. "If you cannot trust me, Jo—how can they?"

She took particular care then, playing down the emergency over her mike. Replacing it in its rest, she caught Hans's approving glance before he indicated the pumps outside the filling station. Together, they sighed their relief.

The small café wasn't of the calibre normally frequented by their Company, but

81

it would suffice. Without prompting from Hans Joanne led her tourists off.

Turning round to see how he was progressing at the garage, she had to stifle a horrified gasp. Smoke from the damaged rear wheel rose to the height of the coach. Hastily, she directed her passengers' attention towards the café's limited facilities. She had them all settled at tables when Hans beckoned her from the door.

"They can only effect a temporary repair here. I have laid on another coach to take you all to Florence."

"Us? You're coming, surely?"

"Later. I've found you another driver. Somebody has to organize breakdown services so this thing can be repaired satisfactorily. At the moment the people we normally use aren't answering, but once I make contact I'll hire a car and head for Florence."

"And if you can't raise them—what then?"

"I'll drive the coach there myself."

"Hans, you can't—you're taking too much of a chance!" Joanne was aghast. But he ignored her exclamation. "Your replacement vehicle will be along within half an hour;

please go and inform our tourists. Then help me unload their baggage."

They worked silently, stacking suitcases outside the café, and—with this possible hazard ahead for Hans—Joanne realized how important he'd become to her. "It doesn't have to be you, have you no sense of responsibility? What happens to your Company, if you meet with an accident? Let the other driver remain here with this coach, you come with us . . ."

The eyes Hans turned on her were lasers. He gripped her wrist. "That is *not* my way! I would never, under any circumstances, order another man to tackle something I dare not attempt. Stop arguing, Joanne—get our clients ready." He started walking away towards the motor mechanic. Sensing she was motionless still, he retraced his steps.

"It's only because I care what happens to you," she declared.

"If so, you will remember you'll please me by considering my Company sufficiently to obey my instructions!"

Again, he turned away, and this time without looking back.

Joanne spent the next few minutes praying something would delay the other coach until she was reassured the breakdown people would attend to their original one. Or so that Hans might travel in convoy with them. But all too soon, she spotted the familiar green and gold livery approaching along the Autostrada. Hans introduced her to Giuseppe, the driver, then helped them transfer the baggage.

"Get everyone aboard now," he said, then added: "and, Joanne . . ."

She looked back over her shoulder. Briefly Hans grinned. "Do not forget it's their holiday!"

Once they were installed in the second coach, he came inside. "You have been patient over the hold-up. I am sure Giuseppe will give you a pleasant journey to help compensate. Plenty of time is allowed for this stretch, so you won't be late for dinner." He gave them a winning smile. "See you in Florence." He stood waving from the roadside until, to Joanne's consternation, her eyes filled with tears and concealed him. She reached for the mike. If she kept her mind occupied, she might survive until anxiety evaporated with Hans's arrival in Florence.

"Let's have a song, Joanne," someone called from the back; "to restore our spirits."

Soon everyone joined in, and Joanne observed thankfully that no one seemed perturbed by the delay. Since her passengers were amusing themselves, however, she was free to worry about Hans—would he have to drive that damaged coach? And if the tyre wasn't faulty—what was wrong? What was going on?

Without further incident, they arrived at their destination, less than an hour behind schedule. Joanne complimented Giuseppe, believing Hans would have done so.

The Italian seemed surprised. "It is my job, no? To move our clients from A to B?"

"Yes, but . . . surely you left something else in order to co-operate?"

Giuseppe smiled. "And will my Giovanna be mad! Today was my rest day. But I am asked to come—I come. You have not work with us much time, have you?"

"No."

"Ah—so. You are not understanding that if something is requested one is happy to comply. We are like a family."

She smiled, pleased by the unsolicited observation.

"Your driver back there said Mr. Lindt,

himself, was concerned all should go smoothly. I hope he will be satisfied."

Joanne nodded. "I'm sure he will be delighted, Giuseppe."

"*If* he lives," she thought, her smile fading as she was overwhelmed by foreboding.

4

JOANNE tried to forget Hans during dinner that night and, afterwards, touring the floodlit city with her clients. Meeting up, as was customary, with her colleagues in a bar near the Ponte Vecchio, however, only accentuated how colourless life seemed without him. Several times she caught herself watching the entrance as if willing him to come.

Sipping her drink, she determined to think about something else—when they got back to the hotel he'd surely have arrived.

And she reprimanded herself for getting into this state—what was Hans to her? He'd only been kind to her, after all, when she'd split up with James. Or had there been more . . . ? Well, if there had, it was simply because the nature of the work threw them together so much.

There was no sign of their original coach at the hotel. Perhaps Hans had been able to leave the vehicle to the breakdown people and continue here by car.

Bidding good night to her tourists and to Giuseppe, Joanne rang the bell at Reception. In a few moments the girl emerged and smiled, recognizing Joanne. "Yes—you wish something?"

"Only to ask which room Hans, my driver, is occupying. I—I have a message for him."

"But he is not here. We think he will not now arrive until the morning."

"Has he telephoned?"

"No—we have had no word."

Forlornly, reluctantly, she went to her room. Was she never to have a good night's sleep? She ached with weariness. She'd left England to escape her problems, only to find herself plunged into a succession of mysteries. There'd been the stranger following her in Amalfi. And the more she thought about Hans's reasons for taking to driving his own coaches the less she believed he'd told her everything. Now, with this damage to their coach, she couldn't help feeling that they were caught up in something sinister. She was certain Hans had been more disturbed than anyone would have been by an ordinary vehicle failure. So what did he suspect . . . ?

At three o'clock, still sleepless, Joanne

stopped trying to see beyond her room to what was happening somewhere on the Autostrada. She reached for her book, but after a few words her eyes went racing ahead of her brain, extracting no meaning from the page.

She flung the book across the room and it skidded on ceramic tiles then fetched up against the long Venetian blind. A faint breeze forced the blind into an irritating "tap-tap" against the book. Annoyed, Joanne padded across to retrieve it; then something prompted her to open the french window, and step on to the balcony.

She smiled wryly at herself. She knew what she admired in Hans. It was the way he never said no—to any task, regardless of the danger, ignoring any possible discomfort. He took the hard way instead of the easy. And if he forced her to do likewise . . . ?

She wouldn't care.

So long as he came back, now, safely. He could go on expecting . . . too much of her—and she'd go on struggling to do all he expected. Always. Even if (as seemed likely) he was never more to her than her boss.

Once—it seemed a lifetime ago already—she had loved a man who had an assured future with his father's company; and he'd accepted that future as his right.

Hans, in similar circumstances, was proof of what he'd once told her—that money, position, make no difference to the person one is. She'd believed then that he was utterly wrong. Now, she wanted only the chance to show him she acknowledged he was right.

Distantly, above the ceaseless hum of city traffic, the uneven throb of a faulty engine obtruded. An expert would have diagnosed the trouble, but she was no expert. As she listened, though, Joanne sensed that this was the car she awaited.

Breath suspended, she continued listening and heard its driver change gear; with difficulty, she thought.

And now the vehicle was surely coming nearer.

She thought it was turning off the road leading from the centre of Florence.

Joanne swallowed, hard, on the lump that had remained in her throat since morning. Then she saw lights as the driver negotiated another corner and came towards the hotel. In the faintly illuminated street she could discern a dark saloon car.

Unable to wait any longer, Joanne seized

her housecoat, flinging it on as she ran. Downstairs she sped, through the sleeping hotel, across the shadowy reception area. She drew back heavy bolts, then ran through the garden. The car was drawing up at the kerb and as it did so its irregular engine spluttered out.

Joanne took her first real look at the thing—heart plunging to her bare feet. The front of the car was smashed in, its windscreen shattered. The offside headlight alone remained, the other corner having been sheared clean away. She hurried to open the door. Hans was hunched over the wheel—motionless. He'd arrived, but at what cost to himself?

"Hans!" She'd intended a tentative, cautious whisper, not the horrified squeak that emerged.

Startled, he glanced towards her and blinked. "Christ!" he exclaimed.

Relieved to hear him speak, Joanne giggled, on the verge of hysteria. "Thank God, you're alive!"

Hans raised his head further, she saw his lips twitch slightly. "Am I?" he enquired drily. "Thank you for telling me!"

She was beside him now, her arms about

his shoulders. "Come on—let's get you inside."

"Presently. Let me recover my breath . . . Lord, what a nightmare!"

Joanne remained motionless, holding him, waiting . . . At last he stirred, turned and looked hard at her.

"Joanne, Joanne—I thought I'd never make it. Had to see you . . . Kept going . . . had to keep going . . ." His voice trailed off. Again, he hunched his shoulders, rested his head against the steering wheel.

"It's not your day, is it? What happened— did you hit something?"

Hans moved, shook his head. "No—no, it was worse than that. I will tell you all about it—later."

Joanne took charge, assisting him from the car and through the garden to the door she'd left ajar. Closing it behind them, she pushed him towards a near-by chair while she locked up, looked in the reception register for his room number and found the key. He managed to walk to the lift, and leaned heavily against its side as they ascended.

At his floor, Joanne took his arm again. "Oh, Hans!" she exclaimed again on reaching his room and, without thinking, hugged him.

For a long time they just stood there, locked together, then she felt his lips on her eyelids.

"Why on earth are you wasting tears on a stubborn man who risks . . . too much, for this insane notion that he'll solve everything himself!"

Embarrassed, blinking tears from her lashes, Joanne moved away. "It's just tiredness—though Lord knows I've wished today you weren't so bloody brave."

"Brave? That is the last thing. I have never been so scared."

"Hans, what happened? You must tell me . . ."

"I will. First, though, will you attend to this?"

His right hand was encrusted with blood, the flesh torn from several knuckles.

"How did it happen? The windscreen?"

"Partly—I had to clear away enough to see out. Mostly, however, it was contact with a somewhat rigid jaw."

"Now I know why your couriers learn first aid!"

Joanne fetched her own kit and while she

cleansed and dressed his hand, he put her in the picture.

"It took an hour, I guess, to get the breakdown people to the coach, so it wasn't that late when I set out after you in the car I'd hired. I'd travelled about fifty kilometres when I realized somebody was tailing me. Whenever I looked in my mirror, I saw this Pinzgauer—similar class to a Range Rover—three or four cars behind . . ." Hans grimaced as she used antiseptic, then continued: "The car hadn't enough power in reserve to accelerate away. I tried hanging back to make the thing go past, but of course he didn't. And every other vehicle went by—leaving the two of us too close."

"And . . . ?"

"It was as good as over—clear of the other cars, he kept edging up on me, till he got me into a slip-road leading from the Autostrada. Then he forced me into a deserted lane. He rammed the car, repeatedly, until it was off the road. He chose his spot—I fetched up, hard, into a wall."

"And this . . . ?" Gently, Joanne raised his hand.

"I could not permit him to drive away."

Hans's lips twitched again. "If his face is half as sore as my hand . . ."

"You left him there?"

He chuckled, amusement overcoming exhaustion. "Should I have brought him along for an introduction?"

"You know what I mean—he wasn't able to drive away?"

"It'll be some time before he contemplates driving. Surprised him—he believed I had lost consciousness with the impact. He sighed, shaking his head. "All the same, I am not made for this . . . pugilism. I was trembling from head to foot."

"Yet you drove here—that was dicey."

"So was hanging around. Besides, I made it, didn't I? After a considerable delay—I couldn't get the engine running."

"You've reported the incident to the police, of course?"

He shook his head and Joanne frowned. "But surely . . ."

"Sit down, Joanne—listen to me . . ." Hans waited while she settled on the edge of the bed. "I've no idea who that fellow was—but I can guess what this is all about. Earlier, when that wheel was examined, the mechanic could not understand why the brakes had seized up in that way. I knew they had been tampered with. This has happened before . . ."

"Hans! You mean . . . ?"

For some time his eyes held hers. Joanne believed he was going to tell her something, but he only shook his head. "It is better you do not know too much."

"Hans, are you safe? Shouldn't you return to your office?"

"No way," he replied, calmly. "I will see this through—then I will return to administration."

"If you live that long."

"Stop fussing. Just . . ." Again, his eyes sought hers, ". . . bear with me. And I'll contact the police when I've something concrete to report instead of . . . suspicions."

* * *

Next morning at breakfast Joanne enquired how he was feeling.

He grimaced slightly and replied, "I'm all right," giving her a conspiratorial grin. She was going to question him more closely when one of the schoolmistresses came fussing towards their table, seeking change. Since Joanne was short of thousand lire notes, Hans took out his wallet. An envelope slipped out, revealing on the reverse the sender's name. *Frau Lindt.*

Yet again, Joanne wondered if Hans was married, but "Frau Lindt" could be his mother, or a sister-in-law. Shrugging away the thought—what business was it of hers, anyway—she forced her attention to sorting change instead. And then the telephone rang, distantly, and a waiter summoned her to take the call.

It was their London office, announcing that the homeward flight was re-scheduled. They'd take off from Berne, instead of Basle, on Saturday and spend their last night near Lake Thun. She must explain diplomatically to their clients, emphasizing the advantages, playing down the irritating itinerary change.

When she explained all this to Hans, he frowned. "Shall I help to break the news?"

About to accept readily, Joanne changed her mind. She wouldn't have Hans believe her incapable of coping. She grinned, shaking her head. "You must step in if you think I'm jeopardizing the Company, but I'd like to tackle this my way."

Hans nodded, appearing pleased.

Apprehensively, Joanne went to the space

between tables and requested everyone's attention. Briefly, she told them what was happening, gave what she hoped was a convincing smile: "So—we'll take another route through the mountains, you'll see different scenery from the outward run. And tonight's hotel is, I'm told, fabulous!"

"What about landing time in England?" Mr. Hughes demanded, showing some of the irritation present that time he'd complained about their room.

Fortunately, Joanne could assure him they should touch down at Luton on schedule. His wife smiled. "Then that's all right. You see, our son's meeting us."

Joanne noticed several heads together in agitated consultation. Someone spoke up. "It won't cost any more, will it?" Eyes dancing, she reassured them. "What's wrong—nearly spent out?" Amid general laughter, she went back to Hans, sensing that she'd won everybody's co-operation. Hans's smile verified this.

"You certainly needed no assistance from me."

Instinctively, she responded to his friendly commendation, for he was proving most amiable. But she'd have to fight the

98

inclination to like him too well. Their encounter was, after all, as good as over.

"It was such a pity I did not arrive last evening," Hans began: "I was going to invite you out."

Joanne smiled—aware that the smile didn't reach her eyes. "I was tired anyway. I'd have refused."

"Since I missed the opportunity, I wondered if we could manage some time alone at lunch-time in Milan. These people will be content to explore after we have eaten."

"I've some shopping to do," Joanne lied, determined not to encourage him. "If you've something that can't be said now, it can wait."

"But this will be our only chance . . ."

"There's still tonight."

"Not for me. I shall take you all to the hotel, attend to the off-loading, then be away. You have not realized, have you, that I shall be almost on my doorstep. Tonight, little lady, I shall have the luxury of sleeping in my own bed."

Despite rearrangements, the day went smoothly. Everyone appeared contented throughout, and Joanne was relieved to find their hotel *was* superb. Although satisfied by this, she felt an aching emptiness, especially when Hans left immediately the last case was inside the hotel.

He had annoyed her also by leaving without first verifying tomorrow's departure time. Talking *en route* from Florence, they had contemplated an eight o'clock departure, but intended checking that an earlier start was unnecessary. She only hoped he wasn't required before that hour.

By the time she'd enlisted the hotel porter's aid in delivering the baggage amassed round the lift to the various rooms, Joanne felt exhausted. Later, in the dining-room, she forced herself to eat slowly, to relax, and to dismiss Hans from her mind.

The meal over, she hurried from the hotel to walk in the Alpine stillness, gazing around her as the setting sun added an ethereal atmosphere. A thin mist swirled about near-by peaks lending a fairy-tale beauty.

Joanne had liked Italy, had enjoyed exploring its magnificent cities and picturesque coastline, but Switzerland she loved.

She stood motionless—although aware of tourists grouped near the tiny church, feeling alone. Alone—with the majestic mountains, sloping pastures, and the tang of the pines.

Curiously, she felt she belonged, the country itself welcoming her, so that even isolated she'd never be lonely here.

Then a door opened nearby, a tall, fair young man emerged, calling gutturally over his shoulder as the door closed. Like Hans, yet unlike, he disturbed her.

Now she was lonely.

Swiftly as she'd left the hotel, Joanne hastened towards it, only to be hustled by her tourists towards the bar. One of the women seized her arm. "Come along dear, this is our last chance to make a fuss of you! You've looked after us well. What are you drinking?"

Surprised, she determined to banish all gloom and smiled round at the holidaymakers now finding themselves seats. From tomorrow she'd have different parties, but none would mean as much to her as this, her first. She moved from group to group, asking how far each tourist would have to travel after touching down at Luton, learning about their families, their homes. She wondered, briefly, if she should have talked more with them earlier, if she'd been too preoccupied with Hans, but their obvious satisfaction with the tour reassured her. Fleetingly, she wished Hans could see their smiles, hear their flattering remarks—if only because he was head of the Company.

A middle-aged man gravitated again to her side, offering another drink. He grinned. "Got to look after you now that driver of yours isn't around. Where's he vanished to?"

"Home. I understand it's quite close."

Henry smiled. "Don't blame him—dashing off to the local birds!"

"Or to his wife . . ."

He looked surprised. "Hadn't thought of him as married. Oh well!" He chuckled ribaldly: "He's been away for a while—imagine making up for lost time—wow!"

Joanne made herself join in the general laughter, but soon made her excuses and went to her room. Her imagination, working overtime already, needed no further prompting.

Once in bed, to her intense annoyance, she found she couldn't sleep. Why? Was she infatuated with Hans? She'd come abroad believing she was in love with James. Maybe that emotion wasn't love, but had she learned nothing from the experience?

Eventually, by reading till almost two-thirty, Joanne fell into a restless sleep but she was heavy-eyed still when her alarm shrilled at six.

*　　*　　*

Henry O'Brien stopped beside her at breakfast. "Wonder if Hans will be punctual? Bet he's exhausted!"

Joanne tried to laugh but failed. She was torn between rising to the bait on Hans's behalf and the unnerving premonition that he wouldn't arrive on time.

She caught herself watching the door while she buttered and ate her roll and drank the strong coffee, willing Hans to appear. As though, in some way, that would prove him unattached. Since the random words had made her doubt that Hans was married she'd been trying to tell herself that she didn't care—to no avail.

Now they'd finished breakfast, and still he hadn't arrived. Fortunately, her telephone call to the office had brought approval for starting out at eight. But it was already a quarter to—and the coach couldn't be loaded until Hans appeared with the key.

Eight o'clock came and went. Joanne

assembled her tourists in the foyer. She watched the hands of the clock tick round to eight-fifteen, sought help to move the baggage to the coach—anything that would save time later.

Returning to the party, she explained Hans had been unavoidably delayed, would arrive shortly, and wondered why she was excusing him.

Joanne was outside, tapping an impatient foot, when the silver-grey Mercedes sped round the square and stopped. Hans sprang out calling a hasty goodbye, in German, over his shoulder—without a backward glance to the flaxen-haired woman at the wheel.

Joanne met him on the pavement. "About time!" she snapped, before his haggard expression and heavy-lidded eyes registered.

Oblivious now of the fact that Hans owned the parent company, heedless of the danger of voicing her opinion, Joanne was conscious only of her indignation.

"I'll make up the time *en route,*" Hans said tersely, not looking at her, striding through the hotel.

"And risk how many lives?" she demanded, running to keep up. "It's . . ." She consulted her watch, forgetting who'd given it to her; ". . . eight twenty-five."

Hans snorted. "It is different now, I notice—when it is not *your* latecoming which has necessitated the hurrying!" His accent, as always, was intensified when he was angry.

Briefly, Joanne was abashed, but not sidetracked. "You're the one who always does things by the book, considering nothing but your precious Company!"

Hans swung round from unlocking the coach. "Strange as it may seem, I am only human—on the rare occasion, I place family needs first!"

Even though, baggage stowed and everybody seated, Hans kept his word, ensuring a safe, rapid drive to Berne airport, Joanne could not forgive him. A heavy silence enveloped them at the front of the vehicle. Disillusioned, she could only be thankful Hans wasn't the driver for her next tour starting that afternoon. Already she was counting the hours to being rid of him.

★   ★   ★

Joanne, who was meeting her new party in Basle, had little spare time after escorting everyone into Berne airport. Emerging, she glimpsed Hans in a telephone booth.

"Already," she mused, "placating that fabulous female to whom he gave the brusque farewell?" Joanne felt sorry for her—subjected to long absences, protracted nights, and hasty dismissals!

Wondering which coach, among the many converging here, would take her to Basle, Joanne looked round, hopefully, for their green and gold livery.

Somebody touched her arm. "Excuse me." The English was spiced with an Italian accent: "You are Miss Kirkham, yes?"

"That's right."

"I am Renato—your new driver. Please come with me—I have already your baggage from Hans."

She ought to have felt relieved at being spared meeting Hans again, but was conscious only of the unpleasant taste lingering from their quarrel. Still, she was starting a new tour, with fresh passengers, and a different driver—how better to forget him?

Renato proved talkative—in Italian, so Joanne had the hard work.

His conversation occupied her until reaching Basle, where she found her new tourists were a jolly, united bunch by the time they'd cleared Passport Control. A good omen! And how she needed one.

The average age was lower than usual, the tour promised to be lively. She could dismiss the mixed events of the past fortnight: this was a new beginning which she was free to enjoy.

★   ★   ★

Getting to know her clients, Joanne warmed to their fun-loving good nature. They treated her as one of themselves, challenging her to delight in their holiday with them. They settled contentedly into hotels, and became, in the coach, positively boisterous, singing when there was no commentary and encouraging songs from Renato and herself.

They enlivened the second night's somewhat dreary Italian town, magnetizing other hotel residents into participating in impromptu dancing after dinner, until, looking around, Joanne felt as if she were a part of some great family.

It was absurd, with carefree companions, to be depressed on arriving in Rome. She supposed this was due to ending her relationship with James here—knew she was refusing to examine the true cause of nostalgia.

That first evening, nearing the Trevi fountain, she shuddered, catching sight of someone familiar. She'd been concentrating on not losing her tourists in the crowded, narrow street, when she felt somebody watching her. Joanne looked to left and right, seeing no one, then felt her gaze drawn to one of the many souvenir stalls. Partially concealed by the flurry of gaudy scarves, stood the dark stranger who'd followed her in Amalfi. And her feet were against the surround of the fountain now, she couldn't escape.

Their eyes met—and held. She thought he smiled. Then, after a lingering stare from amid the silks, cottons and gossamer, he vanished.

Although unnerved, Joanne had no time to reflect on the incident. Her people were demanding explanation of the traditional tossing of coins into the fountain. They teased her because she wasn't throwing in coins along with theirs. But she only forced a smile and turned away. Her mood tonight was anything but sentimental.

Silently bidding herself to cease this

misery, she checked that her clients were ready to return to the coach. Bustling as ever, the area gave up its normal cacophony of blaring horns. Amused last time by the abuse hurled from one incensed driver to the next, today Joanne found it irritating. Then suddenly the atmosphere grew menacing.

Across the road a cluster of *Carabiniere* officers paused on their way back to headquarters; there were murmurs all around of a disturbance following a rally in the Piazza Navona.

Nothing about Rome tonight was conducive to happiness. Or were her low spirits responsible for this apprehension?

Renato was grinning as they moved off in the path of another coach which had parked nearby. She heard voluble Latin abuse, but Renato only laughed. Continuing towards their surburban hotel, she noticed the other coach behind them still—all but nudging them along. Joanne watched Renato's amusement bristle into anger. Approaching the hotel, that same vehicle remained on their tail.

She meant to caution Renato to let the matter drop, but he'd slid back the door so she must help their passengers alight. As the last few headed for the hotel, she looked round for her driver. He was over by the other coach which was stationary now in the middle of the road. Angry voices split the night air. Then the engine started up. Renato began walking away, backwards, gesticulating still.

"Renato, look out . . . !" A car had swung out from the kerb; Joanne couldn't understand how anyone failed to see the agitated Italian. Despite the vehicle's slow speed, the impact made Renato stagger. He seemed about to escape with jarring and shock, but then he half-turned, over-balanced, put out a steadying hand to the car bonnet. His cry was animal-like as his foot went under a wheel. The driver seemed to panic and, gathering speed, fled. As Joanne ran to kneel beside Renato in the road, she glimpsed several pedestrians, trying, vainly, to stop the motorist.

Obviously in agony, Renato clutched his foot, yelling Italian oaths. A taxi stopped and Joanne assisted Renato inside. Tersely, she asked for the nearest hospital.

★　★　★

Long past midnight, Joanne trudged out to the hospital steps. After the seemingly inevitable delay, Renato's foot had been X-rayed and the X-ray had confirmed that various bones were fractured. He would be detained for some time.

She glanced round, hopefully, for a cruising cab, wished she'd asked the hospital people to summon one.

A private car circled the drive and drew up. Winding down its window, the driver smiled. "I saw what happened, outside your hotel. Like a lift?"

Joanne simply stared, unable to find her voice. It was the man in the white safari suit.

"Oh, come on . . ." he persisted, smiling reassuringly, "I'm not after anything. As you can tell, I'm English—from London and a respectable part! The name's Neville—Neville Cushman."

She hesitated. There was no taxi in evidence and riding with him could be preferable to a long, solitary walk—through streets open to stragglers from that disturbance in the Piazza Navona. But she needed to know more about him first.

"I'll take you straight there—you have my word."

"Everywhere I go I find you watching me. And you followed me—in Amalfi. Why?"

The man chuckled—easily, as if to establish *her* ease. "Do you never look in a mirror? You'd find the exercise rewarding!"

Despite misgivings, she began to smile. He'd opened the door . . . the seats looked inviting—and she *was* exhausted.

"I'll admit there are more conventional approaches," he continued, reassuringly, "but you didn't give me a chance to introduce myself."

Joanne supposed that was true. She got into the car, felt his sidelong glance, was thankful when he concentrated on turning the car and heading out on to the road.

Driving along, he enquired after Renato, made sympathetic noises when she detailed his injuries. At the hotel Joanne opened the car door. "Thank you, Mr. . . ."

"Neville," he corrected her, gently.

She thanked him again, got out, and watched him drive away. Well, she reflected, she was here, perfectly safe. There'd been no reason for the doubts she'd had about accepting the lift. She'd probably done the man—Neville—an injustice from the start, and all because he wanted to get to know her.

5

WHEN Joanne phoned Head Office, they promised to get a relief driver to her speedily. Fortunately, as the day was devoted to sight-seeing with a local guide, their coach wouldn't be required early.

That morning, while her holidaymakers explored Rome, Joanne returned to the hospital. She found Renato cheerful enough, though cursing the carelessness that had caused the accident. He'd be discharged soon; his foot in plaster, however, he wouldn't drive for weeks.

By dinner that evening the past twenty-four hours were taking their toll; Joanne felt utterly weary. Devoid of appetite, she toyed with her food.

Looking up as a shadow crossed her plate, she gasped. Hans.

"Hallo." What else could she say?

She didn't smile, nor did he. He looked tired, she observed, as he took the chair opposite hers, but she didn't comment. "Didn't expect . . ." Joanne began, but Hans interrupted, ". . . to see me again? Well—just proves you never know . . ." He sighed. "I don't suppose my arrival here pleases you any more than it does me! Only remember what I said before—in front of the clients, let's not make our mutual distaste too obvious."

This was dreadful. She'd anticipated, after their recent animosity, there'd be some awkwardness in meeting again, but this . . . ! Hans sounded scarcely able to address her civilly.

Next day he remained equally cool. Joanne was contemplating apologizing for her outburst, when Hans sought her eyes across the table. "You may as well know the worst— Renato won't be fit this season; unless we find a new driver—unlikely this late in the year—you'll be with me till the autumn. I'll endeavour to keep out of your way when we're off duty."

Joanne's spirits plummeted. Although reluctant to admit it, she'd been surprised by her instinctive pleasure at Hans's sudden re-appearance. Now he had underlined his atti-tude how could she endure the rest of the season?

Day by day, the tour progressed, uneasily; for though their clients continued happy-go-lucky, Hans's frown hardly ever disappeared. Even the dark glasses he wore constantly failed to conceal the misery in his eyes.

As before, Hans left them in Sorrento, and as before, Joanne missed him—with less reason now their relationship had so deteriorated. And he returned to her equally morose. She longed to ask him what was wrong, ached to win his confidence, but her lips remained sealed. She dreaded learning that her company was the only thing upsetting him.

The overnight stop near Thun had been taken into the itinerary, so she expected Hans would be going home that night.

The journey from Florence completed rapidly, he seemed . . . different. As though he'd reached some conclusion. Placing the last suitcase inside the hotel, Hans gave her a nod, with a trace of their old familiarity; "And so—now I will be going home . . ."

But he didn't leave, appeared instead to be waiting for something. Her admonition, perhaps, to be on time tomorrow. If so, he'd wait for ever; nothing would induce her to comment on his behaviour again!

When she only tightened her lips, Hans

grinned for the first time since they'd met up in Rome.

"I know," he murmured, steering her towards a quiet corner. "Do not be late!"

He was deliberately provoking her, but she could summon remarkable control. Now Hans was looking pensive.

"You could, of course, ensure I arrive punctually . . ."

"How?"

"I needn't go till after dinner—your duty then will be done. The proprietor is a personal friend—will keep an eye on things in your absence."

Joanne was incredulous. "In *my* . . . ? But this is my job."

"And if I assert I need you with me . . . ?"

"Hans, you can't be serious," she babbled. "What will . . . ?" About to demand what the flaxen-haired woman would make of her arrival, she stopped. Surely Hans knew what he was suggesting. And why.

"I could have dinner here, anyway," he added. "Give you time to consider . . ."

He was disappearing towards the telephone when Joanne caught his arm; bewildered, she might be—but she couldn't ignore the intuition that much depended on her response to his invitation.

"Did you mean what you said?"

"I've hired a car, it's a pleasant run, though not very far." His tone was relaxed, but somehow Joanne sensed that Hans had rehearsed it all.

"But, why on earth . . . ?"

Hans sighed. His glance slid away, then he sought her eyes again. "I want you with me. Please, Jo." He made the abbreviation of her name—something she normally abominated— a caress.

"Jo—please," he repeated.

"You'd better arrange things here. Let's be off now—before I think better of this!"

The car he'd hired stood outside. As soon as she'd got her overnight things together, Hans opened the car door for her, then slid behind the wheel. For over a kilometre neither spoke, then Joanne decided to startle him into telling her the truth.

"Won't—won't your wife think . . . ?"

Hans let her get no further. "Wife?"

"Frau Lindt—and don't pretend . . ."

"Little lady, you are very confused. Who on earth would tolerate me? No, Joanne, the only Frau Lindt is my mother—the person we are going to see."

"But that . . . ?"

". . . female who delivered me—late—at the hotel? Okay, in name, she is Frau Lindt—my brother's widow. Klaus died, in an avalanche."

"Oh."

"You do not know me, *Liebchen*, or you would not imagine me married. I am terribly outmoded. I would not leave at home my wife and spend my evenings dancing with another woman—however attractive!"

Joanne swallowed, hard. "I'm sorry."

Light from the dashboard revealed his smile. Hans cleared his throat. "And I, also, am sorry—for worrying you that time, leaving you to cope with everyone, and a driverless coach. Perhaps when I explain you will understand . . ."

"It doesn't matter," Joanne muttered, realizing that it didn't—a cloud was evaporating. Something inside her was singing that Hans was unmarried, and implying a new relationship between them was being established, tonight.

They'd reached a lay-by on the mountain pass. In daylight it would be a vantage point for admiring the lake now reflecting the crescent moon amid conifers.

"Always, since meeting you, I have wanted to talk," Hans began, as the engine died. "At first I told myself that I must not bring further unhappiness to those eyes already sad." He hesitated. Tentatively, Joanne placed a hand on his. Hans locked it with his fingers. "That dreadful day when you said I was too concerned with my own affairs, I had thought . . . of our parting, of never having an opportunity to talk things out with you. On the way down the mountain here, I had decided to take you aside at the airport, to tell you that I couldn't—wouldn't—say to you goodbye. Because, although I could not give you my whole attention, I could no longer exist without your . . . understanding. I intended to say that, somehow, despite your job, despite mine, I had to see you again . . ."

"Hans!"

"You are surprised? And I! A man in my position tries to remain independent. Not too difficult perhaps while it seemed every girl I met was over-impressed by my money! Then you came along to show me what I am really like . . ."

"M'm?"

"No longer self-sufficient because of too many crises. No longer able to sleep, to eat, when worry . . ."

"Tell me, Hans . . ."

He sighed. "I wished to have you understand, first, that I do not want you to share only my anxieties, but . . . perhaps *that* I can show you, with time. Now, if more quickly you learn what eats at my heart, you will see how I need . . . one friend, little lady, to whom I may speak of these hurtful things . . ."

For too long he stared into the distance.

"Yes, Hans?"

"One by one, they have all gone—Father; Klaus, my brother; soon there will be me alone. It is too much—the Company, much work, much responsibility. And at home," again, he paused. "My mother is dying, slowly, certainly. There is no cure, no way even of making life easier for her."

So that was it. "I'm sorry." What could she say to something so dreadful?

Hans nodded, squeezed her hand.

"Years ago, following the war, Mother was ill; they operated, removing one kidney. They told her she would still have a normal life. For some time that was so, we lived in hope, learned to forget, until . . ." Hans stopped, swallowed and continued, "A few years' since I was out skiing; Mother was recovering from my father's death. Elena and Klaus had announced the coming of their child, we all looked to the future . . ." He paused yet again, "Skiing down the next mountain, I saw the avalanche approaching, could do nothing."

"Oh, God!"

"It swept down over our chalet; Klaus died shielding Elena from the rushing snow. They had just got out of the car, you see, outside the chalet. My mother was on the steps, the door open in welcome."

"But she wasn't killed?"

"No?" Bitterly. "To her it was death—a slow, tortured sentence. She was dashed several metres down the mountainside. Among the debris was a sharp rock, which pierced her remaining kidney."

"Hans!"

"How easy it would be if *I* were the one suffering!"

"But is it hopeless? I thought, these days, they could do so much?"

"Kidney graft, you mean? Twice, they have tried. The second rejection occurred recently . . ."

". . . when you were home that time?"

Hans nodded.

Joanne found tears on her cheeks, brushed them away. "And all I did was criticize!"

"You were right, Joanne. My duty was with our clients. Responsibility makes no allowance for feelings."

"You got us to the airport."

Hans shrugged. Presently, he lit a cigarette, offered her the pack, absently. Joanne shook her head. Still not looking at her, Hans went on: "It is so hard being torn . . ."

"I'm not surprised you were miserable away from home." She knew suddenly that no mere disagreement with an employee had kept Hans driving around Europe, in these circumstances. She remembered the damaged coach, hints of other mishaps, and realized Hans was anxious about some threat to the Company as well.

"You understand?" he continued. "It wasn't moodiness, it wasn't—most of all, it wasn't—irritation because of you."

"Or not all the time!"

In the semi-darkness Joanne watched his lips twitch slightly.

"That is what I like in you, Jo, you are fair.

Promise you always will be, with me—give me a chance."

"A chance?"

He smiled, ruefully. "When—*if* I see a way to thinking beyond the difficulties . . ." He fell silent then, but Joanne couldn't leave something like that unfinished.

"Yes . . . ?"

Still holding her hand, he raised it to his lips. "I would wish always to be seeing you—whenever possible."

She gasped and heard Hans laugh.

"After all, there were times—I thought—when you seemed to enjoy my company . . . that evening in Rome, maybe?"

Joanne nodded; "I was remembering—missing you, when you came out there."

"And I behaved badly!"

"And I was embarrassed by all I'd said to you, should have apologized for being hasty."

Hans drew her close, his kiss preventing further words. "So, now you know more about me," he said, eventually. "And we must be on our way."

"What's the latest bulletin on your mother?" she asked, as they continued up the snaking road.

"As usual, she is just hanging on to life—

they put her on dialysis, of course, when the second kidney failed, and there have been subsequent transplants. I had a unit installed at the chalet, so at least she does not endure regular hospitalization."

"Is there no hope of another transplant?"

"Very slight. Her specialist fears she is too weak."

"Who cares for her at the chalet?"

"Mathilde—she's a sort of housekeeper, has been with us for years, and spoils us abominably. She looks after the house as well, and Elena and Kurt."

"Kurt is . . . your nephew?"

Hans nodded. "A fine boy—Klaus would have been proud."

"Elena must be."

He snorted but said nothing.

"Surely, if the boy's all she has . . . ?"

Hans shrugged. "Who knows? Elena is . . . Elena. Unpredictable. She enjoys not conforming. Or, maybe, I have prejudice—Kurt and I are close. Always, he senses when I am at home—you will see, in the morning."

"But he's her son . . ."

"Do not question me, I am not unbiased."

In companionable silence, they completed

the journey. Hans drew up in the wide drive of the large chalet, turned, smiling to her.

"Thanks," he murmured, "for coming."

Mathilde appeared on the steps to be introduced, to fuss over them, before leading the way indoors. Then Hans indicated a door to their left.

It opened on to an exquisite room, traditionally Swiss, with its wooden ceiling and panelled walls, complete with large pictures. A log fire crackled in the grate—Joanne wondered at its necessity, so early in the year, then noticed somebody occupying a large armchair.

A lilac dress complemented the silver hair, but did nothing for the woman's somewhat sallow complexion. As she turned to them Joanne observed the brilliance of her blue eyes—and how they lit up on seeing Hans. Something in his impulsive haste to take the fragile hand brought a lump to Joanne's throat. She'd learned much tonight about this seemingly composed man, but this greatly endeared him to her.

She hung back, near the door, watching mother and son together, but Hans extended his other hand, "Come on, Jo . . ."

Shyly, she crossed to them, found his hand

warm on hers. He introduced them, drew up a couple of chairs: "Now, Joanne, make yourself welcome here, Mother will tell you . . ."

"Why yes, naturally." Beginning in heavily-accented English, Frau Lindt reiterated her son's words. Then, learning Joanne could converse in German, she continued, "You are so talented! In my day a girl was taught little besides keeping house. You modern ones have my admiration."

"Joanne is a better linguist than I shall ever be," Hans asserted. "And quick to learn. Her new job did not set her many problems—as I was telling you."

Joanne looked from one to the other. "Hans is much too kind—he's made allowances for many faults."

His mother laughed, "*Him?* Never! He has told me how good you are—*and* how warmhearted."

Joanne gazed, astonished, at Hans, but Frau Lindt was speaking again, proving—despite ill health—extremely alert. Until Mathilde came in to announce dinner, conversation never faltered.

"We've not yet shown you your room!" Hans exclaimed. "How appalling!"

Joanne smiled. "I hadn't given that a

thought. If you tell me where to freshen up, I won't keep you all waiting."

"You've a lovely home, Hans," she remarked, crossing the hall, "and a wonderful mother."

Joanne noticed the empty place at the table, saw Frau Lindt's eyes linger there, but nothing was said.

Soup over, Mathilde was serving veal in an aromatic sauce when the door was flung open. The fair woman Joanne had seen in the Mercedes paused on the threshold.

"Oh—you!" she exclaimed, seeing Hans, then appeared to look through Joanne.

Hans rose, introduced them, waited for his sister-in-law to sit, his expression devoid of a smile.

"Haven't you kept soup for me?" Elena snapped at Mathilde, who was offering vegetables to Hans.

Joanne watched the housekeeper stiffen and take a deep breath. "You shall have soup directly, Madam," she responded, smoothly enough, though she didn't hurry, hovering first at the sideboard.

Frau Lindt and Hans were frowning. Elena alone seemed unperturbed. Attempting conversation, Joanne smiled across, "Hans tells me you have a son . . ."

"Kurt, yes," Elena replied, without pursuing the topic.

"How is he?" Hans asked, hastily, as if to fill the silence.

"Boisterous, as always!"

"Does he know I am staying the night?"

"He will."

Again, Joanne tried to make Elena respond. "I noticed how expertly you handled the Mercedes, when you drove Hans to the hotel."

Elena shrugged, "Oh? I didn't see you."

"Elena . . ." Frau Lindt began, warningly.

"Yes?" Elena's hard eyes challenged her to criticize.

"Oh, nothing, dear—nothing."

Thus the meal continued. Joanne was disappointed; earlier, she'd been delighted to be with Hans and his mother, but now everything was changed.

The meal ended, Frau Lindt rose, slowly. "Now, I'm afraid I must retire to bed—such a stupid time, but there it is. Soon Mathilde will have me settled—I hope, Joanne, that Hans will bring you to me. I must rest, but that does not mean I must vegetate! I shall enjoy learning more about you."

Hans took Joanne to her room, leaned against the door-frame while she hung out the few things she'd packed before leaving the hotel.

"It is good to see you here, Joanne. Repeatedly, I have imagined . . ."

"Imagined?"

Hans seemed embarrassed, "Er . . ."

Elena, passing, interrupted, "You've put her in the gold room then?"

"Mother has, yes. What of it?"

"That is significant, no?" Elena's mocking gaze held his; Hans sighed, swung on his heel. "In ten minutes, Jo, I will return for you."

Surprisingly, Elena came inside and looked round, smiling. "What happy memories! This was my room—before I married. I visited the chalet frequently, scarcely a weekend went by . . ." She wandered, fingering ornaments, toying with the carved clock's pendulum. "What fun it was—everyone knew I'd marry into the family. But I kept them guessing—until the engagement. Only three people knew who would be the one. Hans or Klaus."

If expected to comment, Joanne was disappointing Elena, for speech had been startled away. She'd been surprised, nevertheless, to learn Hans had ever felt more than sexual attraction for this hard woman.

"Oh, yes," Elena persisted, "it had to be one of the Lindt brothers for me, nobody else measured up."

"I was sorry to hear about your husband," Joanne said.

Elena's back was turned, so her voice alone could reveal her feelings—and that lacked all emotion. "One takes what comes. I am accepted as family, this is my home. Before long, however, Kurt will need a father—things will change. You will see tomorrow how I mean, when Hans and my son are reunited. For them, already, exists that special relationship." Elena faced her, smiling, though her eyes were not. "A simple ceremony between Hans and myself will put everything right."

Joanne felt shattered, tossed from the heights to which her spirits had soared that evening.

When Hans returned to take her to his mother, his eyes told her he noticed the difference in her. And when his arm went

130

about her shoulders in the familiar gesture, she believed it was because he understood how Elena loved to cause trouble.

Only Frau Lindt's vivid description of Hans's childhood dragged Joanne's thoughts from the confidence Elena had shown that he would eventually marry her. As it was, time and again Joanne had to force her attention back to the quiet bedroom.

How could Elena be certain Hans would be hers? Hadn't he, only hours ago, told Joanne *she* was the one to whom he was turning for understanding? Hadn't he shown he intended their relationship should develop?

Joanne watched him, sitting beside the bed, his mother's hand again in his, his eyes riveted on her face, as though memorizing every line—against the time when he'd no longer see her. How could so sensitive a man ever be happy with the calculating Elena? Yet she'd inferred that Hans, as well as Klaus, had sought her. It did not make sense.

Joanne sighed. If her presence here was to benefit Hans or his mother, she must dismiss the conundrum.

The sick woman's eyelids drooped, she breathed deeply, gave a tired little smile. "I am sorry—last night I was connected to that wretched machine, tonight I must rest."

Joanne sprang to her feet. "Good night, Frau Lindt; I'll leave you and Hans to say good night to each other."

"Jo—you needn't." Hans was at her side, his arm round her. "I brought you here to share you with my mother."

"Of course." Frau Lindt beckoned from the bed. "When a man like Hans speaks incessantly about a girl, it'd be a poor mother who didn't recognize that girl was special. I am delighted you are here—and we would exclude you from nothing." The thin, cool hand clasped Joanne's, bringing back the lump to her throat.

"I am happy tonight, I will sleep soundly."

"And I am pleased—very pleased—Hans invited me." Instinctively, Joanne kissed the parchment-like cheek, then was compelled to turn away.

"Come . . ." After hugging his mother, Hans put an arm about Joanne's shoulders, guiding her from the room.

Outside the door, she covered her eyes. "I'm sorry, it's just so . . ."

The arm tightened around her shoulders. Hans was leading her, she sensed a door opening, then closing, behind them. She was held, her head against his chest, while he stroked her hair.

All at once, Hans pushed her away. "Stop crying, Jo—or I . . . and I am supposed to be the man around here!"

She forced a wan smile, watched the grin return to Hans's face. He looked tired, but nodded approvingly.

She saw this was his bedroom. Hans sank on to the bedside chair, indicated another chair beside the window. For ages he remained silent, obviously distressed. Joanne longed to comfort him but wasn't sure how.

Eventually, staring down at his hands, he spoke. "You saw then, how . . . bad it is to have someone you love die before your eyes?"

"Yes, Hans."

"Thank God you are with me."

"But you weren't alone before," she protested.

"M'm?"

"Elena."

"What has she said?"

Joanne couldn't reply.

". . . that she and I are close?"

She nodded.

"She has told you how she imagines it was—how she might have become my wife?"

"Yes." And might still.

He rose, swiftly, came to seek her eyes. "Never! Never under any circumstances." His accent intensified: "Always, she make me mad telling everybody this, even while Klaus lived. This simply is not so. She wanted to marry one of us, she . . . requires this kind of background. She does not—how do you say—give in? Sometimes, when she and Klaus were not speaking, she . . . used me. But I, no—*Gott im Himmell*—I could not respond to her."

Reassured, Joanne would have let the matter rest, but Hans seemed determined to clarify everything. "And today? Did she say that I am Kurt's father figure?"

"Something like that."

"You see how well I know Elena. Do not worry, *Liebchen*, I have heard it all before." He dropped a light kiss on her forehead and extended a hand. "Come, I must provide an interesting evening."

"Just a minute." Awkwardly, Joanne went on. "Thank you—for being so frank. It's early days for you to be explaining away other relationships."

"It is necessary," Hans corrected, firmly, "that you may understand exactly the situation." He drew her to him, kissing her thoroughly and was smiling when they moved away from one another. "And," he added, with a nod towards the bed, "this is no place to linger with you!"

Laughing, they went downstairs. From one room came the sound of a piano. Hans frowned. "Elena. Let's go into the study."

Joanne hesitated, listening. "She plays well."

"But of course! She is efficient."

"Don't you mean accomplished?"

"I mean what I said. If Elena determines to achieve something, it will be achieved— efficiently."

"Then shouldn't you be afraid, if—as you claim—you've no wish to marry her?"

Hans laughed, "*I* also have great determination. And it is, even today, the man who makes the choice."

It was, nevertheless, difficult next morning to remember Hans's reassurances. Breakfast was scarcely on the table when a flaxen-haired youngster darted in to hurl himself upon his uncle. Their conversation in German, too rapid for Joanne to follow, was halted while Hans introduced his nephew.

Kurt shook hands, solemnly, speaking at a more considered pace. She responded to what appeared a very adult welcome from so small a child, her pleasure fading as Elena swept through the door.

She came immediately to stand behind Hans's chair—the smile fixed, a possessive hand going to his shoulder. "Ah—so . . ." she sounded delighted, though her eyes remained expressionless. "My son has found his second father again—all is well."

Joanne caught her breath as Elena leaned forward to kiss Hans. A kiss which he manoeuvred harmlessly on to his ear.

"Yes," Elena affirmed. "Our Hans is home—our family is complete."

Rising, succeeding in removing her hand from his shoulder, Hans said, "Your chair is over there. And our breakfast is becoming cold."

Contemptuously, Elena eyed their plates of bacon. "Our visitor is honoured. We are sharing her extraordinary liking for a cooked meal this early in the day."

"Elena . . ." Hans began but Elena, seated

now, was smiling as if to melt the butter on her roll.

"Darling," she protested. "You know I love to tease. If . . . er . . . Joanne, is it? If Joanne is around long enough she will become familiar with our ways."

Kurt, claiming his uncle's attention again, was allowed to hold the stage until it was time to leave the chalet.

"Mother will be sleeping still," Hans told Joanne as they went towards the car. "I do not disturb her when I depart so early."

Kurt, intent on waving from the chalet steps, was joined by his mother. "Come back safe, Hans," Elena called. "We need you."

"Forget that, Elena—it convinces nobody!"

Joanne was startled by his unabashed honesty, but Elena, unperturbed, hugged the reluctant Kurt until they had driven off.

Hans laughed as they headed towards Lake Thun. "Perhaps now she will believe I see through her." He reflected briefly, then added: "Elena gets away with too much; when Klaus was killed she came near to having a nervous breakdown. We all made allowances for her—somehow, that has continued. For too long."

Joanne, nevertheless, still dreaded the

possibility that Hans's obvious affection for Kurt might ultimately bring him to contemplate Elena's schemes. Since, however, he seemed more relaxed at last she decided to concentrate on encouraging the mood.

He grinned as they approached their hotel. "You see, this has worked admirably—we are early! And, to be serious, I am delighted our differences are settled. For the first time in years, I am seeing that even if—when—my mother's painful life is ended, my own life must continue."

Touched, speechless, Joanne placed a sympathetic hand on his knee. Hans chuckled. "Ah—that is nice! What a shame you cannot sit so close in our coach." Joanne was going to withdraw her hand, but he slid his, briefly, from the wheel, preventing her.

"You are not astonished that I respond like a man to your touch?"

*　　*　　*

Since the previous tour the flight to Luton had been retimed for the afternoon, allowing their clients more time touring Switzerland.

During the morning they stopped for coffee at Einsiedeln; so that everyone might see the

Abbey church there, Hans said—although, later, Joanne suspected the long detour involved in taking in the place was largely for her benefit.

While their tourists were drinking coffee still, Hans took her arm and led her towards the building. Nothing about its exterior, not anything she'd seen in any church or cathedral anywhere, prepared her for what she saw inside.

She gasped and stood motionless, gazing round the magnificent baroque interior. Over-ornate some might call it, with its gold and brilliant colours bright against the stark white of the walls; but here was the ultimate beauty as some men, once, had seen it. Here was their ultimate offering. Joanne was moved to the point of tears; with anyone but Hans she'd have tried to hide her emotional response. But he only looked at her and smiled, gently, affectionately, and took her, silently, from the Chapel of Grace to the Choir, with its elaborate Abbot's throne and so round the entire church.

Before leaving they paused again by the black Madonna of the Hermits in her silken robes and as they turned away Hans said, simply: "Father brought me here when I was young." As though that explained a great deal.

"Thank you," Joanne whispered, as they emerged, and found she couldn't say any more. But she couldn't help thinking that no one, no matter what their faith or lack of it, could remain unmoved by such an experience.

By the time they had had lunch in Lucerne and continued on to Berne airport, she was feeling utterly in love with Hans—and with his country.

He parked in the line of coaches outside the terminal building, and as usual requested that everybody remain seated whilst baggage was loaded on to the special airport conveyance.

She was singing happily to herself as she jumped from the coach and went round to join Hans at the rear.

He had just unlocked the capacious boot and was staring into it, horrified. "Christ— not again!" he exclaimed, running a hand through his hair.

Every suitcase had disappeared.

6

JOANNE gasped disbelievingly.

"Hans!"

"What do I tell them? How the hell explain myself out of this?"

He strode to the luggage compartment in the vehicle's side. That, too, was empty.

"Oh, darling," Joanne began, "what are we to do?"

He shrugged, shaking his head. "Heaven knows—whatever I do or say will make no difference; they will be justifiably vexed."

Again, Hans went to the rear, apparently unable to credit what had happened.

He sighed, then straightened his shoulders, walking so rapidly to the front that Joanne could not keep pace. "I am afraid you will be angry," he was beginning, when she reached his side; ". . . as I would be angry in your place. Somehow, I do not know how, your baggage has been stolen. Not one suitcase remains."

Hans waited, letting them exclaim—as he

had known they would—then he requested silence.

"I can only tell you, on behalf of the Company, how sorry I am—and that the baggage compartments *were* secured. I will do everything possible to locate your possessions and return them to your homes."

"Yes, but when?" one man demanded.

"How?" asked another.

"How do you expect us to manage until then?" an elderly lady at the front enquired.

"Yes—how?" came the general cry.

"We haven't unlimited clothes," a young mother added.

So they continued, singly and in chorus, voicing their indignation. Again, Hans heard them out.

"I am aware this couldn't have happened at a worse moment," he went on as Joanne indicated her watch.

They exchanged a glance, and he sighed.

"If you delay further, you will miss your flight. I will start investigations immediately—you have my word. I shall not spare myself until everything is recovered. We have your addresses, with the number of cases you brought along—we will contact you. Meanwhile, I will notify our insurers to expect

142

massive claims. Would you inform either Joanne or myself now if addresses have changed since the tour booking, ensure that you know the insurance procedure . . ."

During the brief respite before meeting their new tourists, Joanne noticed how Hans had aged—how easily one *could* pale beneath a tan. He sank on to the front passenger seat, head in his hands. "God, what am I to do! Last time was bad enough . . ."

"Last time—has this occurred before?"

He looked up and nodded: "Though not on this scale. A few cases went missing—from the side compartment of a coach."

He gazed after their clients drifting dejectedly through the airport doors. "There goes one lot of tourists who'll never again use our firm! Worse, they'll not keep quiet—within days this will be all over the newspapers—in England, then over here. Companies go out of business, *that* they cannot always avoid; but this . . . this is nothing but carelessness!"

"But you said—the boot was locked."

"Of course, but who will believe that? If you did, Joanne, you'd be the only one. To the press, our competitors, would-be clients, we have committed the cardinal mistake. And there have been too many mishaps . . ."

"You mean things keep going wrong—as you hinted after that trouble with the coach? Hans, what is going on? What're you wondering about all this?"

"I'm not wondering, Jo. I *know*. Somebody is out to get us off the road. They've had it in for us since . . ." He glanced quickly at his watch. "*Liebchen*, if you don't hurry, you will not be there to shepherd the next group—off you go . . ."

"But, Hans, you look ghastly."

"Go on—that is an order." He rose, slowly, wiping perspiration from his neck. "And *smile*, don't forget."

★　　★　　★

It was late that night before Joanne managed another private word with Hans—after too many exacting hours. As instructed, she had beamed over their new tourists, struggling to laugh at their jokes and to make conversation, while she settled them into their hotel. And then somebody suggested a party in the bar, to get to know one another.

Joanne had tried to make the party go—

144

despite worrying, for Hans was out trying to enlist the aid of the police.

His eyes were heavy, his face drawn, when he eventually came in. Joanne's admiration increased rapidly as he forced himself to play the entertaining host. Never before had she observed such animation, never had he found so many amusing anecdotes.

Spent, Hans slumped into a chair, after waving off tourists towards lift and stairs.

"How did it go?" Joanne enquired.

He shook his head. "No joy. The police, naturally, will help. But they were frank—it is an impossible task. They are examining the coach for finger-prints and so on. They will not find any. This is a professional job, for high stakes. They will not have made the slightest error. This was planned, thoroughly— we shall not see that baggage again."

"You're so sure! And what you said before—about other mishaps . . ."

"Come up to my room," Hans interrupted. "We cannot talk here—I trust nobody now, must trust nobody."

* * *

"Before I forget," Hans started, closing his

door behind them. "Take this—" He'd extracted several thousand lire from his wallet.

"For what?"

"Replacing some of your own things. We lost our belongings also, excepting hand luggage. You must kit yourself out for the rest of this trip . . ."

"It's all right, Hans, I can draw on my own account." Joanne offered him back the money.

"No." He closed her fingers over the notes. "Please, Joanne—I cannot do a thing to help the others, yet. But *you* I will help."

Hans crossed to stretch out on the bed, then lit a cigarette, inhaling deeply. "You really believed me, didn't you, Jo—when I told you it was some driver's challenge made me take to the road."

"Well—almost. I did wonder if that was the complete explanation. But, well, I thought it was something you might do."

He laughed, drily, "The grand gesture? Perhaps. But it was more than that . . . Towards the end of last season things began to go amiss. We had several injuries, couriers as well as drivers, creating staffing problems. Late in the season nobody wants to join a travel firm. Well, we survived—thanks to a tight schedule, and the co-operation of my employees. I have a loyal crowd, I'll never cease being grateful."

"And the . . . incidents continued?"

"Correct. First a coach came off the road—that could have been dreadful; fortunately, only the driver was aboard. And he had guts—he kept at the wheel to see the thing through a town, then he jumped clear moments before it crashed. The enquiry suspected that somebody had tampered with the vehicle. It was after this one of the other drivers gave me his opinion of people who sit securely in an office. I decided then to have a go, myself at . . . solving the problem."

"But how—without knowing who was behind it?"

Hans glanced towards her. "I thought I did know. Last year, a rival company made a bid to buy me out. I told them, adamantly, I was not interested. Afterwards, these . . . incidents began. Everything pointed to this competitor. I found it hard to believe, he is a tough businessman but . . . Anyway, eventually, I could endure no longer the suspicions. I invited him to meet me, faced him with it."

"What did he say?"

"He was aghast that anyone should employ

such tactics. I could tell he was speaking the truth when he denied all connection with the . . . occurrences."

"So . . . ?"

"I am convinced this is the work of someone with similar motivation—someone totally unscrupulous!"

Far into the night, they talked, trying to unearth a possible lead to the instigators of this latest *contretemps*; then later seeking some way to prevent the inevitable bad publicity which would result when the news leaked out. But to no avail—they seemed powerless.

At three o'clock Hans told Joanne to go to bed.

"While you're awake—worrying yourself ill? Not likely!"

"*Liebchen*, please. One of us must remain alert."

But Joanne, her eyes misting, only shook her head. "I can't leave you, Hans—not in this crisis."

"Then lie down—here, beside me." Hans grunted, ruefully. "Lord knows I couldn't be less of a threat to any girl, even you! Problems this size play havoc with the rest of my life."

Joanne must have slept, however uneasily; it was daylight when she opened her eyes. Hans, shaving, turned to smile.

"Morning," he greeted her, coming across. He bent to kiss her, "I'm lucky, Joanne—I knew that before, you've proved it by the way you wouldn't leave me."

"We're in this together."

"So it seems. And I had something better in mind when asking you to see more of me . . ." Again, he kissed her, then frowned. "There is one thing, Joanne. If the worst happens and I am forced out of business—the Hans Lindt you've known is very different from the fellow he will be if this lot goes *kaput*. It would break me, Jo; Father built up the Company, I exist to keep it going, to expand, on his foundations. Without that . . ." He shrugged, sighed. "Think about it, seriously; there might be money still—but nothing in which to invest—no ambitions."

"Hans," Joanne began, firmly. "You won't change that much. You've made a good job of driving—you'd succeed at anything. I'll battle every inch of the way beside you to keep the Company going. But if we're beaten you won't go under, you'll fight back."

Hans started protesting, but Joanne was going. "I'd better dress."

He called her back. Hands on her shoulders, he gazed anxiously into her eyes. "Look after yourself—be wary. Renato was hurt, remember—another incident, I am thinking, which wasn't accidental!"

★   ★   ★

The news broke. London office rang through to say a Sunday paper had given the missing baggage banner headlines. Hans was dejected but Joanne, if possible, more upset. The newspaper involved was owned by James's father. Although adverse publicity from another source would have been equally disastrous, she hated having this connection. She was puzzled too: certain the Sundays would have gone to press before their tourists arrived back in London.

Hans agreed. "It is all part of the plot. Whoever arranged disappearance of that baggage had the story ready for some editor."

"Then you've got to do something . . ."

"Are you inferring I'm doing nothing?" he snapped, only to apologize. "But do not get on at me. I must handle this my way."

Restless, in her hotel room on Monday night, Joanne had an idea which she alone could try. Although it would have to wait, and must be kept from Hans, it could unmask their troublemakers.

When, half-way through the tour, Hans flew back to Switzerland, Joanne's anxiety about their relationship returned. Despite his straightforwardness about visiting his home while she remained in Sorrento, she felt uneasy. She could picture him, all too vividly, at the Lindt Chalet—and could visualize Elena making up to him.

She was unable to concentrate for long on anything but that wretched woman—and Hans's undoubted affection for his nephew. Disconsolate, she walked that evening to the town's *piazzale*, and settled at a café table.

She sipped her drink, miserably, scarcely looking about her.

"Cheer up—it may never happen!"

Glancing up, Joanne failed to identify the speaker.

"Sorry, I . . . Oh, Stella! Didn't recognise you immediately. I was thinking . . ."

"I noticed! I hope the gloom isn't occupational."

"On the contrary; the job's proving . . . interesting."

Stella laughed. "What—with the boss himself as your driver?"

Joanne was bewildered, until recalling that Hans had mentioned that Stella was in the picture. Stella put a finger to her lips, conspiratorially; "I know—I looked all round for eavesdroppers. The secret's safe with me."

"But how did you know *I* know?"

"Ah," Stella smiled, mischievously, "the great white chief himself! Happened to meet up at Head Office in Berne. Naturally, I asked how you were coping. He's delighted with you—but couldn't resist a chuckle at your expense—about that form, and your expression on learning his identity!"

"I can imagine!"

Joanne had to smile to herself, wondering what Stella would make of their developing relationship.

"He's all right, isn't he, Hans? As you said—*when* you know him."

"Somehow, I thought you'd take to him. No one else has all season. They say he's too interfering—for a driver. I guess that's true."

152

"I think he's out of his element, driving. And lonely."

Stella contemplated her, quizzically, then sat beside her. "You're not getting involved are you, Joanne? Watch it—you won't have seen the dame who drives her Merc. She's quite something!"

Joanne longed to explain that she'd met Elena, had been told all about her—that she meant nothing to Hans.

"But there it is," Stella continued, "every decent bloke has some female in tow. The grape-vine has it Hans is shopping for a ring. Good thing he can afford the sort that'll satisfy that bird!"

No! Something inside Joanne screamed. She stifled her protest. It isn't true—he feels nothing for Elena—nothing. So he claims.

Although Stella changed the subject, Joanne could not let it alone in her mind. She stayed with Stella only long enough to ascertain whom she must contact to find another courier to cover for her while she took a couple of days off. Then she returned to her hotel room.

Even though she had dreaded Hans's eventual engagement, she hadn't contemplated it this soon. Why had he, only so recently, denied any relationship between Elena and himself? Why bother to draw Joanne into his family circle when he was on the brink of marriage?

He didn't need her, did he—not in these circumstances. She would do one last thing for Hans, though, because she believed she knew a way to reveal who was harassing his Company—and she did care, a great deal, about what happened to it, about what happened to him. He hadn't deceived her, he'd only shown the reluctance of many a bachelor—protesting, to the eleventh hour, that he cared little for the woman in question.

Joanne spent ages weighing Hans's words and behaviour against Stella's news; failing to make them balance. One thing alone remained clear—her introduction into his home had been a mistake. Hans's affection for Kurt and strong family feeling made sense of any move to unite the Lindt family more closely.

She was listless next morning at breakfast, after her alarm had startled her from a brief, uneasy sleep. It was an effort to smile, exchanging pleasantries with her tourists, making an early start for the sea trip to Capri. Joanne wished only to leave them in the capable hands of their local guide, then return to the hotel and sleep.

The sun was blazing down already when their coach, from a town centre hotel, arrived, and she installed her party aboard. She resisted the temptation to leave them with Annetta, the other courier—Hans wouldn't approve such delegation of responsibility. Besides, the harbour wasn't far—soon she'd hand them over to the guide, and come back here.

Joanne stepped from the coach at the harbour, almost into the arms of Neville Cushman. Instead of the safari suit he wore cream trousers and a coffee-coloured silk shirt, which, she had to admit enhanced his tan and dark hair. She'd never been so aware of the intensity of his brown eyes, the length of those near-black lashes. Had her interest in Hans made her forget his existence? Certainly she no longer mistrusted him.

Swiftly, Joanne collected herself, as he exclaimed delightedly: "Ah—my friend! I heard you were in Sorrento, hoped we'd meet again. How are you? And your driver— Renato, wasn't it? Has he recovered?"

"I believe he's now recuperating—at home,

somewhere near Genoa. I've not heard much since he left hospital."

"Of course." He looked towards the vessel at the quayside. "Come along, they're almost ready . . ." There was something over-whelming about his assuming charge of her. If she'd been flattered by his undisguised interest, she'd still have deferred encouraging him until she felt less tired and better able to cope.

"Oh, I'm not going across. There's Vincento, our tourist guide—I must take my people to him . . ."

Neville whatever-his-name-was, however, smiled charmingly towards her tourists. "Do you permit your courier to sit alone in the hotel while you enjoy Capri?"

They invited her along, of course, and her new companion insisted: "We won't take no for an answer. Surely for one day you can relax—see something of the place."

"I'm desperately tired, I'd intended to rest."

"I know just the spot." He was leading her to the quayside: "A villa belonging to some friends—they're away, and told me to use it. Ramon, their man-servant, will provide lounging chairs, cool drinks . . ."

Despite her resolutely-shaking head, Joanne was hustled aboard, settled on a seat shaded by an awning and hemmed in by her holidaymakers.

First one then another remarked on the pleasure of having her with them. It would be churlish not to enter into their mood; churlish, too, to refuse the drink which Neville offered. Lemonade. It was refreshing after her turbulent night. Joanne started to unwind as the engines throbbed into life. She leaned back, aware that somebody was moving along to accommodate her escort beside her, but she was determined to remain unresponsive. Maybe Cushman, was it? had won this round, getting her aboard against her will, but she'd have her way the rest of this trip. She'd meant to sleep, she'd do precisely that—here, to the soporific movement of the vessel; on Capri, in the shade somewhere. And if she recovered sufficiently to explore the island, she'd confound him by seeking the company of her tourists!

She dozed, off and on, gazing occasionally from beneath her lashes, then—finding him present still at her side—feigned sleep again.

She must have slept, soundly, and was startled awake by shouts and something striking the boat's stern. Opening her eyes, Joanne discovered they'd reached Capri and small craft were jostling about, intent on ferrying people to the Blue Grotto. Reminded of the visit to that other cave, the Emerald Grotto, where Hans, fooling, had drawn her close, she shook her head when Neville urged her to transfer to a rowing boat. Men were all alike, and she was fast becoming tired of their idea of fun!

"But you must," he persisted. "Everyone does . . ."

"I shall be the exception—I've no intention of . . ."

But she had to leave her seat so others could pass and was swept into the crush to the side of the vessel. She clung on, but he touched her arm. "One moment, let these Americans through."

Joanne released her hold. Too late, she realized he was steering her towards the swarthy boatman holding his small craft steady. In the throng she couldn't move from the side and, suddenly, strong arms were hauling her, like it or not, over into the rocking boat.

Oarsmen and tourists alike were laughing; Neville prevented her retreat. As he squatted behind her, on the inadequate seat in the wet boat bottom, she was certain he gave some sign to the boatman. Presumably, to indicate they should go. She sighed ruefully, "Do you always get your own way?"

"I should be so lucky!"

Ashamed, momentarily, of her seemingly unsporting reaction, she turned round, "I really was tired—wanted to be left alone."

"So you shall," he promised, a hand on her shoulder, "once we reach the Villa Circada."

As she faced forwards, Joanne gave a startled cry. They were heading away from the rest, rounding a rocky promontory. The boatman, shipping his oars, coaxed a motor into life.

"This is most unfair!" Joanne exclaimed, loudly—hoping to attract attention, but already the engine was whipping the boat through the sea—out of earshot of everybody.

"Don't be alarmed," Neville began. "You requested opportunity to rest, I'm ensuring that."

"Oh, yes!" she responded, sarcastically, "I'm sure!"

"God, are you suspicious! What's the matter with you—can't you look after yourself?"

"Of course." Coldly.

"Then let go. Do you suspect every man you meet of evil intentions?"

Joanne drew in a breath, but he forestalled her. "Just because your driver's a foreign boor . . ."

"He's not!"

"Oh—like that, is it?"

"Like what?" Joanne demanded.

His chuckle infuriated her. Recovering somewhat from the shock of her abduction, she made herself smile, deciding to work on the boatman. In fluent Italian so he couldn't mistake her intention she requested to be put ashore.

She intercepted some signal between him and Neville.

"I am sorry," he replied, in English as good as her Italian. "That is impossible here."

"Back to the Blue Grotto then," she pleaded, "or to the ferry."

"I am sorry."

She glared over her shoulder. "Do something, can't you? Make him take me back."

"I will," Neville assured her, serenely. "When you have rested—you'll be at the harbour for the same boat as your tourists."

"You don't know what time."

"Don't I?"

Joanne realized she wouldn't be surprised if he knew all her arrangements. He appeared from nowhere with alarming frequency.

"You shouldn't be impatient . . ." He pointed along the coastline. "Here's the Villa Cicada—already."

Spurning assistance, Joanne leapt ashore the instant the boatman tied up at the jetty. As swiftly as loose shingle permitted, she stalked off, up the track.

Laughing, Neville came alongside her. "You make a grand gesture of independence. I don't understand why—but I like your spirit."

Joanne snorted.

"That, however, is *not* attractive."

"Blast you!" She stopped and swung round. "You've engineered this—can't you be satisfied! Leave me alone."

"You have my word. Once I am assured Ramon is conversant with your needs, I'll disappear. Until it's time to leave."

"Then why this elaborate plot to make me accompany you?"

Neville sighed, eyes serious. "I'd intended, hopefully, we'd spend the day together. I've told you I'm attracted. But forcing my company on any girl goes against the grain. So . . . you get your way."

In silence, they crossed towards the tree-shaded lawn, clinging to the slope below its villa. Joanne heard the boat zoom away. Neville indicated garden loungers, in the shade, beside a white wrought-iron table. Calling "Ramon!" he vanished, to return with a small, dark-eyed man, in pristine jacket over dark trousers.

"Miss Kirkham," Neville announced, smiling coolly, "who will spend the day resting." Stepping back, he watched Ramon set down the tray laden with drinks and glasses.

"I hope you have all you require, Miss Kirkham," Ramon said. "I'll bring food later. If there's anything else . . ." he demonstrated the small brass bell, "I shall hear."

"Do sit, Joanne," Neville insisted. "I thought you were tired."

"I'm not stopping."

"Please, Miss Kirkham," Ramon persisted, "at least, sample our hospitality—you must be thirsty."

Joanne swallowed, forced her eyes from the

ice, clinking still, in the tall glass Ramon offered. It was hot today, and she was parched . . .

Now he plumped the lounger cushions, adjusted its shade, looked to her.

She glanced towards Neville—to discover him walking away, quickly. Sensing her gaze, he waved a casual hand, without turning. Joanne shrugged; it couldn't hurt, could it, to sit—briefly? To recover her breath, to calculate her next move. Again, she eyed the inviting glass and pointed to an empty one. "You taste it, Ramon."

Smiling wryly, he half filled the glass, raised it to her, drank deeply. "You see . . ." he said. Then left.

She sank on to the lounger, which was as comfortable as it looked and then reached for the glass.

She detected gin, well balanced with lime—and sipped thankfully. She'd been frightened by the sudden spurt of an engine in that tiny boat, by dashing round the coastline away from everyone. Soon, she'd be herself again—fortified, would be on her way.

Her glass was empty, except for a last ice cube melting into a tasteless puddle. Her eyes were magnetized by the tall glass jug—its temptingly green-tinged contents indicating it was a similar concoction.

Cautiously, Joanne poured a drop into her glass and tasted . . . She nodded, topped up, the ice tumbling chattering from the jug.

She lingered over this drink, her head against soft upholstery. Sensing somebody watching, she glanced to the house and noticed Ramon at a window. White teeth flashed in his bronzed face as he smiled approvingly.

That was all very well but, observed, how could she steal from the villa—make her way to the town? She suspected Ramon had been briefed to detain her. She angled her chair affording a view of that window; once he moved she'd leave, hurriedly.

For almost an hour, she waited, alert for any movement from the villa. At last, Ramon left his observation post, crossed a sun-terrace, disappeared through a narrow garden-door, which slammed behind him.

Joanne caught up her shoulder-bag, and sped beneath the trees. Running through, she found herself beside an artifical stream which bounded from rock to rock in a series of waterfalls, running down the hillside towards her.

Her eyes traced it to its apparent source—a tree-fringed pool. Beyond, a high wall enclosed the estate. Smiling to herself, Joanne scrambled up the path beside the stream. This was going to be easy. And, away from the Villa Cicada, she'd find her tourists. Capri wasn't that big. Somebody would direct her to the harbour; she spoke the language, could enlist aid. She'd wait then, the rest of the day if necessary, for a familiar figure. Because nothing would induce her to return alone to the mainland.

Experience had proved Neville was expert at shadowing. Anywhere, on Capri, aboard the ferry, in Sorrento, he could find her.

He might wish simply to become better acquainted, but he'd have to be satisfied with their one encounter today.

The heavy door in the wall wouldn't yield. Annoyed, Joanne removed her sandals, attached them to her bag. Barefoot, she'd more easily scale the wall. Several crannies offered toe-holds, space for her fingers. Pleased with her resourcefulness, she reached for the smooth stone topping the structure.

Baying and barking, the dog sprang, from nowhere. Teeth fastened on to her ankle and he pulled.

Her fingers scrabbled, fruitlessly, at the smooth wall top. Grazing legs and arms, she fell, rolled several metres, to sprawl on her back. Growling menacingly, the enormous dog planted stout paws either side of her head.

Joanne started inching her face from its slavering mouth. The dog snarled. Scared, she tried to turn on her side, to wriggle away. Jaws snapped, near her ear and hot breath steamed her cheek. Again, it bayed—head thrust high.

Seizing her chance, she flung herself sideways, toppling the animal into a yelping heap. But quicker than her, it was up before she escaped.

Teeth found her shoulder. Joanne screamed, piercingly, and again . . .

Frighteningly strong, the beast was dragging her, head first, before she could get to her feet. Stones tore at bare limbs, gravel embedded itself in her hands as she clawed frantically for some anchor. Something struck her head. A rock, which she seized.

Joanne felt flesh tearing before the animal let go. It snapped again, at her wrist, making her loosen her grip of the rock.

Suddenly, they were in the water, both

floundering, though the dog, on its feet, held the advantage. Joanne scrambled, splashing, to unsteady legs. Snarling, the creature sprang, balanced on hind legs, thumping great forepaws on to her shoulders. Briefly, it seemed they executed a grotesque dance, but she was backing away, towards stones edging the pool; she stumbled . . .

Her body was tossed from rock to rock, as she plunged with the waterfall.

She heard herself scream but was silenced as her head struck a tree.

7

"OH God!" someone exclaimed, kneeling beside her. "Ramon!" the voice called.

Joanne opened her eyes, to several centimetres of coffee-coloured shirt.

"Thank goodness!" Neville cried and called Ramon again. "It's all right," he murmured. "It's all right."

"The . . . the . . . ?" she stammered, terrified.

"Dead. The dog is dead, Joanne."

"But . . ." She didn't understand; couldn't understand—not anything. Why, how, the dog was dead—nor what Neville was doing here. She stirred and he shifted, easing her head on to his lap. She saw the revolver then, in the grass, and knew about the dog.

She heard running feet as Ramon toiled, panting, up the slope.

"Bring a lounger or something," Neville suggested. "We'll have to carry her."

"Christ!" he exclaimed, as Ramon went dashing away again. "You are in a mess,

Joanne. But don't fret, I'll get you medical attention. They'll clean those wounds, X-ray for broken bones, administer the necessary jabs."

She nodded, weakly. "Thanks."

Neville leaned over, kissed her forehead: "Thank goodness your face isn't even scratched. I'd never have forgiven myself if . . . Joanne, believe me, I didn't expect this. Thought you'd come round to enjoying a day on Capri, accept that I wanted only to get to know you, that . . ." She felt him shudder: "Joanne—look at me . . ."

She raised her eyes to his and read concern in their brown depths. Attempting to reassure him, she moved, winced.

"Keep still. We can't be certain, till you're seen by a doctor, that there's no internal damage . . ."

"I don't think there is—I'm just cut and bruised all over, and . . ."

". . . torn to shreds where that creature attacked you. Oh, my dear, I'm so sorry."

His sincerity impressed her. How badly she'd misjudged him earlier. Of course, she believed his explanation of bringing her to the villa. She managed a smile.

"Don't go on about it—I suppose it was

partly my own fault. If I hadn't mistrusted you, you wouldn't have gone off—none of this would have happened."

Before Neville could reply, Ramon struggled up with the garden lounger. Gently, they lifted Joanne, then carried the makeshift stretcher down the rest of the slope.

"Shall I telephone for the doctor, sir?" Ramon offered.

"No, I'll take her there—probably quicker. Is the car round the back?"

Ramon nodded.

Joanne rested in the shade until Neville drove round the villa in an Alfasud. He seemed anxious because she couldn't lie comfortably on the back seat, but she protested that she'd be perfectly all right sitting in the front.

Within minutes he had secured her seat-belt and started the engine. "Sure you're all right?"

"Very comfortable—surprisingly so, in so compact a car."

"Lovely little job, isn't she? I was telling my friends recently I intend getting myself one of these. They go like the wind—and, boy, are they a joy to handle!"

Despite her approval of the Alfa, Joanne found the journey painful and hair-raising, as Neville sped over the narrow road snaking up the escarpment to Anacapri, with a near-aerial view over colourful Moorish houses.

Waiting for the doctor, Joanne started to feel sick and imagined this was due to shock. She was about to warn Neville that she was going to be horribly ill when the medico appeared. She took a deep breath and told herself to continue breathing steadily to check the nausea.

The doctor, after a quick glance at her, poured something into a glass and listened while Neville related what had happened. He scowled, noting Joanne's raw palms out-stretched for the draught. Neville held it for her while she sipped.

The examination took time, and Joanne was shivering now in her saturated dress but the medicine calmed her stomach. The doctor spoke no English so she was thankful her Italian enabled her to follow what was being said. Neville, too, she observed, understood every word.

It transpired—to her relief—she would not be hospitalized on Capri; an outbreak of dysentery had brought an influx of patients.

Since no bones appeared to be broken the doctor wouldn't expose her to possible infection.

"When I have dressed these wounds, you must rest while your clothing is dried out, then you can return to the mainland. Tomorrow, you must attend hospital in Sorrento—I will contact them, so they will expect you. I will give you the injections, the rest can wait. I am certain the X-rays will confirm only that there is no concealed injury. Take things easy for some time—but the hospital will give you further instructions."

Joanne had to steel herself not to yell when he injected the anti-rabies serum into her stomach, but the worst was over then.

She must have dozed afterwards in the darkened room at the rear of the surgery; it was late afternoon when she became aware that Neville had reappeared to take her to the boat.

Neville's arm about her, Joanne was even able to laugh as they went aboard. "If any of my tourists see me they'll wonder what on earth I've been doing!"

He agreed, then glanced at the time. "I

don't believe they'll be on this, though; they should have left ages ago."

Once on deck, Neville insisted on finding her something to eat, pointing out that her last meal was breakfast.

"But I'm not hungry."

"You must try something," he insisted, finding her a cushioned seat.

He returned with sandwiches, and a large brandy. "I'm determined that when we reach Sorrento you'll have lost that awful pallor. Now come on . . ."

Joanne tried to eat, but after only a couple of bites pushed away the plate. "I'm sorry, Neville, I can't . . ." She reached for the glass. "This is welcome, though—just what I need." After the brandy she was less aware of the soreness of her wounds. She smiled, "I feel much better."

"And your colour's returning. I'll get you another . . ."

"Do you think you should?" Joanne enquired, giggling. "Remember I've had no food."

"I can always carry you, if necessary!"

Joanne sat back, contentedly, while Neville went to the bar; the brandy had dulled anxiety as well as pain. The whole incident seemed trivial now; she was beginning to wonder how she might avoid visiting the hospital.

With the second drink, her euphoria increased and Neville, apparently relieved, laughed with her, encouraging her as she became garrulous about James and their broken engagement.

Eventually, a sudden jerk revealed that her injuries were *not* magically healing. She grimaced, "What was that?"

"We've reached the other side, that's all." Neville helped her to stand. "You're recovering, I can see! Your cheeks have plenty of colour—but for your dressings and ruined frock nobody'd guess!"

"I'll look a sight on my way to the hotel."

"I'll see you safely there," Neville insisted, putting an arm round her as they left the vessel. "You don't think I'd abandon you? I'll soon find a cab. And in the morning I'll pick you up, take you to the hospital, and afterwards . . ." He turned to smile at her, "I hope you'll let me give you a splendid lunch. I must make amends—if you dare accept . . . ?"

He was helping her across the gangplank; she'd to concentrate carefully on the operation. Her legs, weak before, were

174

seemingly now controlled by some other person!

Again, Joanne giggled. "Do you know," she announced, rather loudly, "I believe I'm drunk."

"Never mind. I'll look after you."

She leaned against him, enjoying being supported—letting someone else take charge.

"You're being extrem . . . extremely kind," she said, trying not to stumble over every word, as he helped her through the crowd.

Joanne felt she was being watched, critically, and assumed it was because of her apparent inebriation. She decided she didn't care but clung to Neville's arm, still giggling. "You're not like I imagined. Fancy me thinking you were up to something!"

"You're reassured then?"

"Absolutely."

"And you will lunch with me?"

"Lunch, dinner, you name it!"

"Excellent!"

Joanne watched Neville's indistinct back merging with the throng, after he'd leaned her against the harbour wall while he located a taxi. Embarrassed by her bandages, she thrust the wrist behind her, pressed the other throbbing palm against her side. The shoulder, though, was agonizing; as was the site of the anti-rabies jab.

"Joanne!"

With difficulty, she raised her eyes past the elegant suit, to focus on a bronzed face, fair hair, above furious blue eyes.

"Hans!"

He said nothing yet. He turned a tiny package over and over in his fingers. Then glanced down, thrusting it hastily into a pocket.

"You've been drinking!" he remarked—somewhat unnecessarily.

Joanne nodded, mirth bubbling up, irrepressibly. Hans looked so angry—she couldn't wait to see his expression change to concern when learning of today's events. He'd only be thankful her injuries weren't more serious.

"And look at you," he went on. "Clothes in tatters, hair all over the place."

"I . . . had an accident."

"In my country, ladies do not take too much alcohol—certainly not if they cannot remain on their feet afterwards!"

Shakily, Joanne stood upright, trying to keep her gaze steady, before his accusing eyes. "I . . . I . . ." her voice trailed off.

Something puzzled her. "I thought you were in Switzerland?"

His nostrils flared, "I am gravely disappointed . . ."

"You won't be when you've heard," she began, quickly, eager to put things straight.

"Disappointed," Hans reiterated.

"But why did you come back early?"

She saw the cloth move, as he fingered the object in his pocket. He withdrew his hand—clenched. She met his eyes and was bewildered by their sadness.

"Disappointed," Hans murmured, yet again, then—scornfully, ". . . and disgusted!"

He'd gone. She watched as he pushed his way through the people waiting for the boat to empty. She heard a car start up, glimpsed Hans, his face set as he sped up the hill.

Joanne noticed tears pricking her eyes and searched for a tissue.

"Here . . ." Neville proffered a neat, white square. "I saw that. Your driver, wasn't it?"

She nodded. "He didn't let me explain."

"No matter." His arm went about her. "Come on—the taxi's waiting . . ."

They'd reached her hotel when Neville spoke again. "Having quite a go at you, that fellow, wasn't he? You needn't take that from anyone."

"I must—or up to a point—you see, he owns that." She indicated their coach. "In fact, he owns the whole bloody outfit, including the staff—or thinks he does!"

Neville whistled, "You mean . . . he's not . . . !"

"Lindt is the name. Hans Lindt. Mister, heavy-handed, boss-man!"

Joanne fumbled with the door, tears blinding her, suddenly sober and miserable. Neville helped her alight, solicitously.

"I'll come in with you—put him in the picture."

"No, that can wait, Neville—thanks. I've had enough. I'm going straight to my room."

"As you wish. Don't forget the hospital tomorrow. I'll collect you here."

"There's no need."

"There's every need. Do you suppose I won't be worrying all night? And don't forget we're lunching together."

Crossing to Reception for her key, conscious again of being observed, Joanne guessed it was Hans and ignored him. When the lift descended, she struggled with sore hands to open the gates. Strong, familiar, hands assisted.

When Hans opened the gates for her, she stepped inside, nodding silent acknowledgement.

"Jo—you're crying."

She turned away her head.

"And your hands—what have you done to them?"

She refused to answer, was too choked anyway to speak. She stepped from the lift at her floor and slammed the gates on him.

Stalking towards her room, she had the door open before hearing Hans leave the lift and start running in her direction.

When he'd taken her at her word, and left her the other side of her locked door, Joanne undressed, slowly, painfully. She slipped on her nightgown and sighed. The effects of the brandy were fast diminishing; every wound, scratch and bruise screamed agonizingly. She'd never sleep. She found the painkillers she always carried and took three for good measure with a further brandy.

★　★　★

Morning brought an aching hunger, soreness,

and an outsize hangover. How, feeling so ill, could one long for food? She felt she'd never survive the morning on the customary roll and coffee.

Anticipating lunch, Joanne smiled. Neville had been so kind, dispelling her misgivings. She was glad he'd take her to hospital; she needed support and could expect none from Hans.

Her sundry dressings preventing both a shower and bath, she had to content herself with washing; her hands were so raw even that created problems.

She was late for breakfast; dressing had taken an age. She noted Hans's frown, as she crossed to him. Sitting, however, she sensed a changed attitude.

"Joanne," he started tentatively, "perhaps I was hasty last evening—you were injured, were you not? I did not realize."

"It doesn't matter."

"But it does. I must explain how I thought . . ."

"Don't bother," she interrupted, more rudely than she'd intended.

"Oh, now, Jo . . ." he caught her hand, turned it palm uppermost when she flinched,

"I thought so . . ." He claimed the other, "Oh, Lord. What other injuries have you?"

Joanne shrugged.

"Jo—I am asking you—what have you done?"

"Nothing." She withdrew her hands, avoided looking at him. Hans sighed, heavily. "Okay, I misjudged you—always, I am misjudging people. Forgive me . . ."

She wanted to . . . Yet, he'd made a scene, in front of everyone, including Neville. She hadn't noticed him while Hans was criticizing, but he knew most of what had been said.

"Joanne, you are not even hearing me. What has happened?"

"I had an accident." Suddenly she wanted only complete honesty between them. She met his worried eyes, smiling ruefully. "And I had too much brandy—to kill the pain."

"Oh, Jo, Jo! Tell me the worst—how serious are the injuries?"

"I'll survive. Got to call at the hospital for a check-up."

"I'll take you."

"It's all right, thanks. Neville offered."

"Joanne, please, don't go with him. Let me take you."

"It's all arranged. I won't have Neville coming here for nothing."

"It was all right, yesterday, for me to hire a car from the harbour, fruitlessly!"

"Hans!"

"You have me worried ill. The whole party arrives here, and you are missing. So I go to meet you and you are not there; and then you are there, but you are . . . not yourself. And I am angry and you are . . . upset, and . . . and *he* is there. And I am not understanding."

"Poor Hans," she smiled. "Look, love, I've got to dash. But we're both off duty this afternoon, I'll come back immediately after lunch."

"*After* lunch?"

"I promised to let Neville take me out—peace offering."

"And for what must he make peace?"

Again, Joanne smiled, "I'm not sure really. The more I consider it, the more convinced I become that I should be apologizing . . ."

"Apologizing?" he interrupted: "To *him*? For what?"

"Not realizing earlier how gallant he can be."

Hans sprang up and, glaring down at her, protested: "Joanne, stop this—before it gets

out of hand. Do not lunch with him, do not—
please.''

''Why ever not?''

''Be careful, Jo. You don't know the man.''

''Do you?''

Hans sighed, shrugged, then strode from
the dining-room.

$$\star \quad \star \quad \star$$

''Neville,'' Joanne began, *en route* for the
hospital, certain she'd be reassured, ''why did
that dog attack me?''

''He was there to discourage trespassers.''

''But I wasn't . . .''

''You were behaving like one. Don't worry,
I'll contact my friends to ensure they don't
replace him with another, equally vicious.''

Joanne felt better with that, and Neville
whiled away the time between various tests
and X-rays with well-related anecdotes.
Awaiting her final examination, she realized
she had also got things into perspective—
especially her difference with Hans. Hyper-
sensitive, she'd over-reacted to his censure.
On reflection, she saw how things must have
appeared on the quayside. She'd gratify him
by trotting obediently back after lunch. And

would listen to whatever he might say about Neville. Only *listen*, though, for she was convinced Hans was biased.

Neville smiled reassuringly when Joanne joined him just before midday.

"I've seen one of the doctors," he told her. "I informed him you're in my care—just to stop them concealing the truth. Anyway, he assures me that, hopefully, you'll soon be as good as new."

She laughed. "So they tell me—although they insist I return for dressings. And I'll have to remain within reach of a doctor for ages because of the rabies jabs—that'll be a nuisance."

"Painful, too, aren't they?"

Joanne nodded and grimaced.

The restaurant to which Neville took her was old, exquisitely furnished, obviously expensive. Her surprise amused him.

"Don't worry— I *can* afford it!"

Joanne smiled as they settled at a corner table. "I'm sure you can. But you've never told me what your job is."

She observed his momentary hesitation, then he replied: "I run an agency—spares for heavy vehicles, including coaches. That's why I get around so much—I have contacts all over the place."

Joanne was pleased to have some of his background filled in for her. Several little things about his behaviour yesterday still bothered her, but they'd soon be sorted out. Once they'd ordered, she'd probe further, so she could scotch Hans's misgivings. But before she could say anything Neville was speaking. "Forgot to ask—did the boss continue his interrogation?"

"Yes."

"Is he satisfied?"

"He will be—when I've seen him again."

"Are you dependent on the work, Joanne? Tell him what to do!"

"I don't really want to . . ." she paused, continued: "You may as well know his interest isn't solely an employer's. He took me home recently, to meet his mother."

"I see." Neville's dark eyes registered astonishment, amusement, though not, strangely, jealousy. He pondered, leaned across. "But surely, he's *the* Hans Lindt—with the attractive, widowed, sister-in-law?"

"How do you know? You didn't say, yesterday, that you knew Hans . . ."

"I only know of him. But watch it, Joanne . . ."

Another warning. She frowned. "Neville, what have you heard—about Hans and Elena?"

He shrugged, "I'm not spreading gossip—it's all over Europe." And he refused to say more.

Unable to even contemplate the inference of Neville's words, Joanne concentrated, instead, on the meal. It proved excellent—a pity her appetite had gone.

Presently, she felt Neville watching her, met his dark eyes.

"You're quite a girl, Joanne—I'm glad I've met you."

"What—shattered still, after yesterday! Come off it, Neville—the old chat's wasted on me."

He sighed, looked down at his plate then back to her. "Because of Lindt?" He shook his head. "You want to find out more about him before you . . ."

"Drop the subject! Unless you want me to walk out of here."

"As you wish. I've warned you now."

Neville changed the topic; amiably, but too late. Earlier, she'd begun accepting him as an attentive acquaintance; already she wondered if he were just another predatory male. At least, that was what she hoped—otherwise . . . there might be a grain of truth in the rumours regarding Hans.

Suddenly, Joanne felt sick of all men. It was all too much—first, the disillusionment over James, then being whisked away into . . . well, whatever the relationship was with Hans. And now . . . Oh, she didn't know what to believe, or whom! Getting away for an hour or two would be best—but first she must keep her promise to explain yesterday to Hans. That shouldn't take long.

As soon as they'd finished their zabaglione and coffee, Joanne stood up. "It was a lovely meal, Neville; thank you."

"Glad you enjoyed it."

"Must return to the hotel now. Will you call me a cab?"

She wasn't surprised he insisted on seeing her to the hotel, but that didn't alter her determination to leave him after a brief goodbye. Neville was a complication she could do without right now.

"I suppose I'll see you around," she said, after thanking him for taking her to hospital and, again, for the lunch.

"That sounds like a dismissal!"

When Joanne shrugged, he felt for a pen and paper on which he scribbled a number. "You can contact me here until the season ends."

She took the note, to avoid argument, but determined not to ring that number. And now to sort out the next one . . .

Claiming her key from Reception, Joanne was given an envelope. It bore only her name. Puzzled, she tore it open.

Dearest Jo,

As you pointed out, we are both free this afternoon—I have to see you, if only to apologize for my behaviour.

Please, Jo . . .

Hans.

She smiled, in spite of herself, glanced at her watch, turned to the Reception clerk.

"Would you ring my driver's room, please—and tell him I'll have tea with him at four o'clock."

★　★　★

"Joanne!" Hans, awaiting her near the lift, took both her hands gently in his. "I have ordered tea on the terrace, is that all right?"

188

He'd lost all assertiveness, she noticed and followed him. "That'll be fine, thank you."

"How are you?" he enquired, drawing out her chair. "What did the hospital say?"

"They were pleased with me," she reassured him, hoping his genuine concern was denial of the rumour linking him with Elena.

The waitress fussed for ages at their table. "Thank goodness!" Hans exclaimed as she left. "I cannot wait to say . . . what must be said." But then he stopped, disconcerted.

Joanne was surprised, she hadn't expected him to be this perturbed.

"I can only admit to being jealous," Hans blurted. "Therefore, forgetting I should not address you as though I were your . . . your . . ."

". . . keeper?" Joanne suggested.

"Lord, was that how it sounded? Even worse than I feared!"

Joanne rescued him sooner than she'd intended because she was relieved all gossip appeared unfounded. "Let's forget it, shall we?"

"So easily?"

She smiled at him. "All friends have the

occasional disagreement—true friends recover quickly."

"You are willing to make allowances?"

She nodded and began pouring tea. "I suspect if I didn't, I'd be the one with regrets."

As she passed his cup their eyes met in mutual reassurance.

"I could hug you!" Hans exclaimed. "Unfortunately, this is not exactly the time or the place . . ."

"Perhaps later?"

He chuckled. "Nobody else could restore my well-being so rapidly. You have no notion how I dreaded this encounter; reminding myself of my haste—your justifiable anger."

"Forget that now," she insisted and asked after his mother.

* * *

It was dark when they left the dining-room together after the evening meal; having talked the time away since tea they seemed now closer than ever.

"All the time I was at home," he'd admitted, astounding her, "I recalled only how, before, you were there with me. How

I'd believed at last, I never need be alone. Even so brief an absence from you made me . . . lost."

"Hans!" She noticed the catch in her voice; his expression disclosed it hadn't escaped him either.

"What you said before, Joanne—about, perhaps later, there being opportunity to . . ." Falteringly, sighing over his inadequate English, Hans was making a terrible job of reaching the point.

She laughed. "You're not that shy, surely! I'd be disappointed if you were content just to talk!"

"There is a secluded roof-garden . . ."

"Let's go then."

He opened the door leading to the roof, glanced round, smiled. "Excellent—deserted." He drew her close, his lips finding hers, tenderly. "Oh, Joanne—if your injuries had been more serious . . . !"

"But I'm fine—stop fussing."

A glimmer of light revealed his rueful smile. "I cannot—every minute I remind myself to take care—I am afraid to touch you!"

"Er—yes," she agreed, wryly. "That is a

complication! My shoulder's the worst now, keep off that and I'll manage not to yell."

Hans led her to the surrounding wall; Joanne exclaimed at the crescent moon reflecting from the Bay of Naples and Vesuvius silhouetted against the starlit sky.

"How lovely!" She turned, freed from all doubt, seeking his eyes, "And lovely to be sharing it . . ."

Again, Hans held her. "All my life I have waited for someone like you, Joanne—for *you*."

They went to a cushioned seat, bougainvillaea-shaded, where Hans kissed her again.

"Remember I said that night I took you home how I had longed to talk with you? No matter what we discuss, how much you tell me, I cannot know enough. Words can never express the knowledge which comes only through living with someone . . ."

"Hans!"

Could this be real—the enchanted setting, this man wanting to share his life with her?

Her astonishment made him laugh. "There," he reproved, "and I was so serious."

"And solemn?"

"Only if you reject me."

"Reject?"

"If you continue interrupting, I'll never get the thing said! Already, you have made me forget the splendid speech I prepared! It is difficult for me, a foreigner, to get right this . . . proposal."

Holding her away slightly, Hans was awaiting her reaction—apprehensively.

"And I have plunged headlong, because I cannot wait for your answer. I was supposed to court you a little, to . . ."

"Hans! Stop talking—I can't take this in."

"Does this help?" He retrieved from his pocket the package she'd observed yesterday, at the harbour. His fingers fumbled the wrapping and he steadied them, she noticed, before springing the catch. Nestling in velvet was a diamond ring.

"Darling!" she gasped.

Hans laughed, relieved. "Thank heavens! I was afraid you would consider it . . . inadequate."

"Why on earth? It's superb!"

"I searched, at first, for something larger than the one James gave you! Then told myself 'No—Jo is not like that.' So, I chose the ring I wish to see on my wife's hand, along with something plain—in gold."

Incoherently, Joanne hugged him, offered her hand so he might slip the ring in place. Again their lips met and his sensitive fingers caressed her.

Presently, she moved slightly, to look into his eyes.

"Hans—this was why you hurried back yesterday, wasn't it?"

"Was it?"

"Don't pretend. I recognized the package. Darling, you'd every right to be . . . disappointed. Sorry I was in such a state."

"Not your fault. I know now—and not to become irate each time I see you with another man. I cannot chain you to my side. Your job entails meeting people." He grinned. "That doesn't mean I shan't try to be possessive."

Joanne smiled, and returned to his arms.

★　　★　　★

Nearing the end of the fortnight's tour they again left their tourists in the care of the hotel proprietor, and Hans hired another car for the journey to the Lindt chalet.

"Do they know?" Joanne enquired, somewhat anxiously, as they started up the winding pass, "about us?"

194

Hans shook his head. "Not yet. I was too unsure that you would accept me. For all I knew, you still longed to return to James."

"Not likely! That was ended aeons ago."

"A matter of weeks!"

"Longer than that—before I left England, only I wouldn't admit it."

"Even so, I was not sure of you at all."

"Yet you bought this ring . . ."

"A token of my own certainty. If you had refused, I would have kept the ring, reserved for you."

On arrival at the chalet, Hans paused only to ask after his mother's health then seized Joanne's left hand, thrusting the ring before Frau Lindt's amused eyes.

"This is mine! Joanne is mine—almost. She . . . she has accepted me, Mother."

Smiling, Frau Lindt kissed them both.

"Joanne, I could not be happier. For years Hans has been too much alone. He has to work hard—and that he enjoys. But everyone needs someone with whom to share leisure hours, plans for the future. Without sharing, that future is empty."

Hans smiled, "Since meeting Joanne, Mother, I have understood why you urged me to think beyond the Company."

Elena introduced the only discord when, late again for dinner, she glanced sharply from the champagne glasses to Joanne's ring, then to Hans. Her eyes questioned him, more acutely than she'd attempt verbally.

Undeterred, Hans beamed. "Yes, Elena—congratulate me; Joanne has consented to marry me."

Joanne watched Elena's steely eyes betray her fury before she lowered their lids.

"Congratulations, Joanne—you have achieved a great deal, very rapidly!"

Joanne felt indignant colour rising, and longed to rush from the room. Hans placed a restraining hand on hers. His mother inclined her head, approvingly, and smiled.

Taking a deep breath, Joanne responded, softly. "Thank you, Elena, I'm delighted Hans has chosen me."

Only later, alone with Hans, did she express annoyance. "That woman! She always finds something scathing to say."

"*Liebchen*," Hans interrupted, hugging her, "do not let her distress you—everyone knows Elena. If she weren't Kurt's mother, I'd not have her here. Remember, you are the one I love."

Joanne gave herself to enjoying this return

visit to the Lindt chalet, until they left next morning, delighted by his mother's plans for a full scale celebration during their next stay there.

As they drove away, nevertheless, Joanne realized suddenly why she was glad she would not see Elena again for two weeks.

It wasn't only that she feared this woman could come between Hans and herself. It was the growing recognition that she wouldn't trust Elena—ever. There was something ruthless about her—something totally unscrupulous.

8

ALTHOUGH their new tour began normally and continued uneventful all the way to Rome, Joanne couldn't throw off the uneasy foreboding that something else would happen to Hans.

He tried to laugh away her apprehensions when she voiced them to him, but she sensed that he, also, was unnerved by the succession of crises which they'd faced.

Even the prospect of their being together in Sorrento didn't reassure her. "You'll be flying back to Switzerland, won't you?"

"Maybe I am not going to Switzerland this time," Hans began, sounding somewhat evasive. Then he chuckled. "One day, little lady, you will know all the time that I am safe—but you will *never* be safe—from me!"

He was more serious, however, about her need to take care. "I am not satisfied that incident on Capri was pure chance." But Joanne would not have that. By the time they reached Sorrento, indeed, she'd dismissed the occurrence. Her wounds had almost healed now, and the hospital tests revealed no trace of rabies in the dog involved. And now she was fit she must get on with discovering who had been behind the disappearance of the baggage—*if* Hans gave her the chance . . .

Two days passed and still he remained. Wonderful though it was seeing him daily, spending free time getting to know him better, Joanne couldn't forget the scheme which was being thwarted.

And then at dinner Hans appeared wearing his city suit. Joanne tried to conceal her relief.

"You're going home then? Give my love to your mother."

"I . . . I may not manage to see her," he responded vaguely.

"I see." Surreptitiously, Joanne wiped sticky palms on her napkin, hoping she didn't appear unduly concerned. "When do you expect to return?"

Hans, amused, raised an eyebrow. "Are you checking on me? Time enough for that when I am your husband!"

Joanne tried to laugh with him, though she felt ill-at-ease. For once in her life she just wanted him to go. Then she could get on with her own plans.

Next morning she breakfasted long before her tourists, and left to take up the cancellation she'd obtained on a flight out of Naples.

The plane touched down, fifteen minutes behind schedule, in a miserable English drizzle and at lunch-time her taxi set her down in Fleet Street.

Wishing she'd consulted her mirror in the cab, Joanne smoothed her brown hair and hurried through the plate-glass doors. The commissionaire recognized her instantly. "Good morning, Miss Kirkham—seems a long time since we saw you; you're well . . . ?" Without awaiting a response, he crossed the hall to lift a telephone receiver: "I believe Mr. James is in—I'll tell him . . ."

"No!" She took a step forward. "I mean, no thank you—I'll go straight up." She reached the stairs before the man could stop her. Nothing must prevent her from seeing James. His secretary, fortunately, was going out to lunch.

"Is anyone with Mr. James?" Joanne asked after they'd exchanged a perfunctory greeting.

The girl shook her head.

Taking a deep breath, Joanne knocked on his door.

200

"Come . . ."

She paused just inside his office, waiting for him to look up. James always presented the top of his head to anyone entering—implying concentration on vital matters, she supposed. How ridiculous, she thought, but without smiling.

"Good God—Joanne!" After the exclamation, he recovered smoothly. "How nice—do sit down . . ."

"I'd rather stand, thanks—this shouldn't take long."

"Joanne—after all this time! Do sit. What is it?"

She remained standing. "It's not a social call, James. Ordinarily, you'd never have seen me again, but . . ." She fumbled in her bag. "I want some information please—about this . . ." She tossed a newspaper cutting on to his desk.

Briefly, James scanned it then glanced up, his face impassive. "Well?"

"Who gave you that story?"

"Can't remember—one of your tourists, I imagine."

Joanne shook her head. "Try again, James—I don't believe it was. This would be going to press when they arrived in London."

"My dear girl . . ."

"I'm not *your* anything!" Joanne started, furiously, before remembering she required something of him. "Sorry—I meant to be impersonal . . ." She paused. "James—please . . ."

Epitomizing the suave businessman, he rose. "Let's go and have a bite to eat, somewhere where we can talk more comfortably."

Joanne swallowed back her refusal; she must play along—at least until she had the necessary information.

He took her to The Cheshire Cheese. At any other time she'd have found the place fascinating. He wouldn't permit any discussion until they'd ordered and were sipping sherry.

"Now, let's be civilized . . ." James began.

"Discreet as well, so long as you tell me."

"Joanne—you know a journalist never reveals his sources . . ."

"You're no journalist; you don't go after a story yourself."

"You're splitting hairs," James responded, softly, making her admire his cool. "And wasting time—my occupation isn't your concern."

"Only when it destroys the life work of people who'd make ten of you!"

"Joanne," he continued gently, his hand covering hers as it lay on the table, "let's begin again, shall we—where you came in . . ."

"So that's it!" a voice roared, behind her chair. "This is your reason for enquiring if I was going to Switzerland! What a gullible fool you have made of me!"

She had no need to turn, no need to look—there was no mistaking that voice—or the accent, thick in its owner's intense displeasure.

Determined to show no emotion before either of these men, Joanne stumbled from the room, down the narrow staircase and out into the lunch-time crowds.

* * *

Indignation carried Joanne the length of Fleet Street into the Underground, then forward to the Air Terminal. There she retreated to the cloakroom, indulged her pent-up tears in a cubicle, then emerged to verify her travel arrangements.

Her return flight to Naples wasn't for several hours but she made for the airport, nevertheless—eager to put some distance between herself and Hans as well as James.

She had calmed somewhat when her flight was eventually called. Whilst regretting the fruitlessness of visiting James, she'd become philosophical about his lack of co-operation.

The thing she couldn't bear was the way Hans had misjudged her. There must be, she supposed, some reason for the doubts he'd voiced, but they'd shattered her. She felt nauseated still, remembering. Did Hans trust her so little that he believed she'd run to James? If so, there was no point to their engagement.

Miserably, Joanne mounted the steps and went into the aircraft. She had a window seat and stared, without seeing, over the tarmac.

Without noticing, she started her old habit of twisting the ring on her finger. She swallowed, hard. She wouldn't cry in public. The plane was filling up—somebody'd taken the seat next to her.

"Leave the ring, for now—remove the thing and you'll only lose it!"

Oh Lord! She'd never contemplated Hans being on this flight.

"Hans," she began, her voice pitched low so it wouldn't tremble. "You'd better take this . . ." Staring straight ahead, she wrestled with the ring, "Since you think so little of me!"

"Later, if you insist." His restraining hand was icy on her fingers. "But I refuse to live out my traumas before this . . . this audience."

Her eyes fixed ahead still, Joanne persisted. "How could you believe I'd sneak off to James to revive whatever relationship there'd been, when you and I . . ."

"I said *later*, Joanne—I do not intend discussing my affairs in this aeroplane!"

A passenger in front of them half-turned, smirking.

"You see," Hans muttered, "you will make me a curiosity!"

"But you won't listen—I'm telling you I went to James about your Company's interests."

"If that is true, you must know I prefer to keep my business matters private—this is no place to air them!"

Taking a book from his document case, Hans opened it—as if closing the conversation. Joanne observed, however, that he didn't turn one page before they touched down at Naples.

Although late evening, the heat struck her as they crossed to the airport building. Despite her efforts, Hans was beside her still as they queued at Passport Control.

"I have a hire car waiting," he stated, evenly. "Assuming you are returning to the hotel—at least to give me notice—you may as well ride with me."

"It doesn't matter, thanks." The flight had proved an ordeal. Prolonged, his disapproval would snap her control. A fool she might be—she wouldn't give Hans the satisfaction of learning she was an emotional one!

She sensed his shrug; he didn't argue.

The moment Joanne cleared the Control area, she hurried through the crowded lounge. The day's expense had been astronomical—a taxi would scarcely make any difference!

Arriving outside, she frowned. Not one cruising cab appeared, nor was there the usual hopeful line of passengers. She spotted the newsvendor's headlines announcing a taxi-drivers' strike. Wearily, she trudged along the exit road towards the main highway. Sometime, there'd be a bus for Sorrento—wouldn't there?

She must have covered a kilometre when

the car drew up. She needed no glance to identify the driver.

"Get in," Hans ordered, tersely, "albeit reluctantly! Even my company must be preferable to that trek!"

"Hans, you've got to listen," Joanne began, earnestly, once the car was gathering speed.

"I'm listening . . ." He sounded as exhausted as she was feeling.

"There was no personal reason for my visit to James . . ."

"Perhaps then you were there to collect settlement for that splendid story about my Company's carelessness in losing all that baggage!"

"Stop!" she shrieked. "Stop this car."

"I will do just that—the instant I find a suitable place. I have no wish to endanger my life, nor the lives of innocent people by driving while I tell you my opinion of you!"

Seconds later, Hans drew off the road, leaned across her and fiddled with the door catch. "Only to ensure you do not leave before I have finished!"

Joanne gulped, still fighting the wretched tears which sooner or later would win.

"I wondered how somebody had got the news to an English newspaper that quickly.

Even those intent on ruining my Company would have had to be slick. Today, it all fell into place. I had not known before that your ex-fiancé was influential in the press world . . ."

"Hans! I couldn't do that—least of all to you. I flew to England today simply to try and learn more. I knew James's paper had released that story—I thought I could make him tell me . . ."

"But there you were," Hans interrupted, "holding hands . . ."

"We were not! He took my hand, that was all . . . just to say . . ."

"'Let's begin again, shall we?'—I heard. It's no use pretending . . ."

"He only meant begin again on the conversation—because I lost my temper when he refused to reveal the source of his information." Joanne paused, reflecting. "Hans—why were you in London?"

"I, too, knew which paper released details about that baggage. I was after the source."

"Yet, you can't believe I'd the same reason for going! Can't you get it into your head that I do care—desperately—about your firm, about *you*? That I'd do anything to help you!"

In the light from the dashboard, his weary

expression seemed to soften. He sighed. "I guess that would be too easy. Life doesn't work out like that. And then there was the underhand way you went about it . . ."

"I've had enough," Joanne began vainly wrestling with the door catch.

Hans's fingers closed on hers. His eyes, still, were cold.

"Why conceal your intention, Joanne?"

"Wouldn't you have stopped me going, if you'd known?"

Slowly, he nodded.

"There's your reason then. Anyway, now I know just how you rate me!"

"That is not so. I simply suffered a . . . misapprehension."

"Sure—I heard! And if you expect me to forgive and forget you're in for an outsize disappointment! Nobody—not even Mr. Almighty Hans Lindt—can say what he likes to me."

Again, Joanne fumbled with the door catch and this time it yielded. Snatching up her bag, she almost fell out of the car and started running along the verge.

"Come back . . ."

Joanne ignored the command. Stumbling over dry tussocks of grass, she fled. She wouldn't return to the hotel tonight. She'd put up in the nearest village. First thing tomorrow, Hans would have her resignation—by cable if that was the only way.

She heard the car door slam and tried to run more quickly. Then her foot twisted over a hidden stone. Hans seized her by one arm and she swung round to face him.

"Don't touch me!" she flared.

Startled, Hans released her. Briefly, they eyed one another, both wondering what would happen next. Joanne noticed Hans looked upset. Well so was she—extremely.

"You think you've only to call me back, don't you?" she demanded. "And I'll come running . . ." Furiously, she beat with her fists against his chest.

Hans remained immobile. In the light from a passing car, she saw his eyes were glinting.

"You're so conceited," Joanne continued. "Conceited, arrogant . . ."

"Arrogant? Oh yes—so *arrogant* that I am not always sure you want me."

"Not want . . . ?" she murmured, confused.

"I dread learning that you're like everyone else—after something. Being nice to me because I am the boss, because I am rich! I have told myself you were the one who couldn't care less about all that—but was I deluding myself, eh? Is it *me* you want?"

"Want . . . ?" Joanne repeated, amazement draining all spirit until she forgot to fight him, forgot to be on guard.

Hans made a grab for her, pulling her against him, crushing her lips with his own. "Want!" he exclaimed, breathlessly. "Need . . . !" He had her by the waist, was propelling her towards the car. There was no escaping him. Noticing her limp, he swept her up into his arms, and carried her the rest of the way. "Don't contemplate running away again, you wouldn't get very far." He opened the passenger door. Then he seemed to change his mind, for he slammed it and opened up the rear.

Joanne looked questioningly at him but he hustled her into the back seat and climbed in beside her. He gave an odd laugh but didn't speak.

"Hans . . . ?"

"This is where I learn the truth—one way or the other."

His mouth claimed hers, fiercely, tongue probing until her lips parted.

A shiver ran through her.

"For too long," Hans announced, pausing

for breath, "I have restrained myself. I can't even guess, today, what you feel for me. But I'll leave you in no doubt of my feelings!"

His blue eyes, laughing suddenly, held hers before going out of focus. His kiss was demanding, uninhibited, cruel.

"Hans! What are you doing? You're not going to . . . ?"

"Do not put ideas into my head. Tonight, I just might consider them excellent!"

His laughing lips again found hers. Despite herself, Joanne was returning his kisses, eagerly.

"You will have to trust me now," Hans remarked, sounding amused still, ". . . *not* to give my emotions free rein!"

He explored her breasts, winning from her a response she'd gladly have withheld—if she'd been capable of withholding. This was no time to reveal how she ached for him. Half-scared, half-excited, beyond heeding apprehension, Joanne found herself stirring and her body, contrary to her resolution, curving against his.

His hands continued their exploration, though gently now, caressing a rhythmic pounding into her veins. Joanne's fingers slid beneath his suit jacket. He slipped out his arms and tossed the coat on to the front seat.

His shirt was silky and thin—Joanne felt the warmth of him coming through. She made as if to draw him closer, but he held her away, briefly, then loosened off his tie, flinging that after the jacket. And now he sought her, dragging her close against his hard body. Through his shirt, unfastened now to the waist, the hairs on his chest scratched the skin above her scooped neckline. But Joanne couldn't move away—wouldn't have done so. She could only draw nearer, lips seeking his again, urgently. One hand found the hair at his nape, the other traced the ridge of his spine.

Excitement increased her pulse-rate, echoing in the vibrating awareness of her every nerve—and in his heart-beat thudding against her. And she was torn between resisting these demands and assuring this loving man of *her* love for him.

Abruptly, breathing rapidly, his smile rueful, Hans drew away. Sitting upright, an arm around her, he laid his cheek against her hair.

"I might have guessed," he exclaimed, "that—fighting like a vixen—there'd be ferocity in your loving!"

"Ferocity?"

"Passion then—passion. Call it what you like! Oh, Joanne—let's not deny this . . . this . . . love?" He hesitated, continued only when she'd nodded; ". . . love we share. We shan't always agree. I am hasty—but I am honest about that. And I'll need constant re-assurance that you want me for myself, but . . . Jo—dearest Jo, marry me! There'll be so much fun, excitement . . ."

"Fun? Excitement?" She was suddenly furious—with Hans for arousing such desire in her—with herself for responding. "Is that all you want?"

"There has been little, *is* little, in my life—apart from this—except reponsibility, anxiety, distress," Hans said, quietly, all joy evaporated.

Joanne touched the lines across his fore-head, ran a finger over his compressed lips before kissing them. "Sorry, Hans. I'm not very understanding, am I?"

"You're all I need."

She shook her head. "But I forget how many problems you have."

"And so you should—your task is to make *me* forget them." He consulted his watch.

"We'd better go, the hotel people will want to lock up."

*　　*　　*

Next morning at breakfast she was bright, animated, talkative. She sensed Hans was amused, felt his unspoken comment.

"So—you are revitalized!" he remarked at last, *en route* for Amalfi. His eyes were on the road ahead, but their glint remained undisguised. "I must remember what makes you sparkle!"

Joanne laughed, quietly.

"You may laugh," he added, "I am serious—I learned a lot last evening!"

It didn't take much, however, to make Joanne forget the morning's elation. She and Hans had lunched with their tourists at a seafront hotel and were leaving, hand-in-hand, when Neville came towards them. He beamed at her, gave Hans a cursory glance, then enquired if she'd recovered from the injuries suffered on Capri.

Joanne was about to introduce the two men, but Hans was walking away, rapidly, towards the beach. She frowned, then gave her attention to Neville.

215

"I'm fine now, thank you. And thanks again for looking after me."

"It was the very least I could do."

He leaned against a near-by shop front, as though intent on lingering. And he seized her left hand, scrutinizing her ring.

"That's not the same one you were wearing that first time I saw you."

"You don't miss much!"

"I try not to! Who's the lucky man, Joanne—is it . . . ?" He nodded to the beach where Hans's fair head was easily discernible among so many dark Italian ones.

"Does it matter?"

Neville shook his head. "I'm sorry, of course, that I'm not the one in favour."

He sounded convincing—Joanne wondered if it hadn't been just the old chat when he'd professed interest in her. She decided it was safer to laugh it off. Taking his cue from her, Neville laughed also. "Well—glad you've got what you wanted."

Joanne left him and hurried to join Hans. She was taken aback by his scowl.

"Joanne," he began, ominously, "I think you should see less of that fellow . . ."

"But, darling, it was only a chance meeting. I couldn't ignore him—he brought me back safely, remember, after the dog savaged me. I can't . . ."

"You *can* make less fuss of him when you meet."

Joanne sighed. This was ridiculous—yesterday it'd been James, now Neville!

But Hans hadn't finished. "You asked what I knew about him—I cannot divulge everything, yet. But there's sufficient for me to mistrust the man. And he was around when you were hurt. You must not get involved."

"I've no intention of being 'involved' with Neville—unless your unreasonable jealousy drives me!"

"Jealousy? It's more than that—it is fear for your safety."

"Rubbish!" she exclaimed. "Admit that's your reaction to any man who speaks to me. Come on, be honest . . ."

But Hans remained silent, disturbing her. Then, leaving his towel on the beach, he strode towards the water's edge and struck out angrily through the waves.

When he returned, however, his good humour appeared to be restored and he insisted on whisking her into a passing cab for the short drive to Ravello.

He put an arm round her as they stood

gazing over the panoramic Bay of Salerno, from the terrace of the Villa Cimbrone. "Please," he said. "Take notice of what I say. Believe me, Joanne, I'm scared something will happen to you. You know how many things gave gone wrong for us this season." He drew her closer, kissed her. "I only want to share life with you . . . scenes like this, whose beauty takes away my breath . . . all the little day-to-day things of which life is composed."

And, standing there with Hans, Joanne felt that same longing to share—and the realization that, for both of them, anything preventing their marriage would be disastrous. She smiled at him and nodded. "Yes, this is good, very good."

And so she was feeling much happier before they returned to Amalfi to meet up with their tourists.

*   *   *

Their days then began to seem idyllic. Joanne found very real satisfaction in working with Hans—part of the Company so important to him.

She had discovered by this time that there

were always similarities between individual members of one party of tourists and the next. There were also, of course, many unique characters, who, because of some eccentricity perhaps, could be likened to no one else. And these added a dash of spice to their tours.

Most of all, though, Joanne simply loved people, and working with them. She couldn't imagine a different life now, and hoped that when she was Hans's wife he would not object to her continuing in this job. She had a suspicion, however, that he would need some persuading before agreeing to such a course. As soon as they were officially engaged she meant to put the suggestion to him.

And their engagement party was fast approaching. She had bought a dream of a dress in Sorrento, all soft and feminine in apricot chiffon, and was describing it to Hans, crossing to their Florence hotel, when he stood still, staring beyond the coach.

"*My* car—over there . . . look . . ."

"Are you sure?"

"Do you think I don't know it?" Passing the Mercedes, he pointed out the Company insignia on the radiator grille. "Proof enough?"

Joanne followed as, frowning, Hans entered the hotel.

Elena, exquisite in a navy trouser suit, rose from one of the armchairs. "My dear," she began, in German, rushing to offer Hans her cheek to kiss, "I am having trouble with Kurt—you know how wilful he can be."

She pointedly ignored Joanne who waited for Hans to include her. She was determined not to be dismissed to her room. Hans glanced at her and then drew her to his side, but still Elena addressed him alone.

"Will you do something for me, Hans?"

"What?" His tone was sharp.

"I have brought Kurt to stay with friends at Fiesole. Would you go over and see him tomorrow—talk with him? He listens to you; he is so much like you."

"Elena—you know I work a tight schedule."

She half-turned away, but Joanne recognized that she had no intention of yielding. "You cannot spare even a few minutes for your family. That is all it will take, dear, that is why I brought the car."

"Very well, I will see Kurt. Give me the address now. We leave Florence tomorrow, I will attend to this immediately after breakfast." Hans extended a hand for the address.

Elena went through her bag. "Oh. It must be upstairs . . . come and get it, Hans."

"Upstairs? You mean *you* are not staying with these friends?"

"No. Kurt needs a break from me. Come on, now, for that address—I am exhausted."

Hans made as if to follow Elena; for an awful moment Joanne suspected he had forgotten her. Then he returned and gave her a hasty kiss. "Sleep well, *Liebchen*—see you at breakfast."

But before Joanne was asleep she was startled by the insistent ringing of the telephone beside her bed. Smothering a yawn, she reached for the receiver.

"*Si* . . . ?"

"Joanne . . ." It was Hans, sounding uneasy. "Will you do me a favour, Jo?"

She laughed. "Depends . . ."

"Come with me to Fiesole. I've a nasty suspicion Elena has something up her sleeve."

"Eh? How do you mean?"

"I don't know."

"All right," Joanne agreed. "I'll come along. What time?"

"That's why I rang you. It means early breakfast. We'll have to be off as soon as you've made sure our people know what time to be ready to leave. We've only just time to get out to Fiesole and back again."

★ ★ ★

"What did you mean, really?" Joanne persisted when she was sitting beside Hans in the Mercedes next morning. "About Elena having some scheme?"

He shrugged. "I do not know. It is simply a feeling, which—with the light of day—becomes more unrealistic. Anyway, here you are. If nothing else it shows everyone where you belong."

Joanne grinned, glancing over her shoulder. "You should be safe, she isn't lurking in the back seat!" She leaned her head against the head-restraint, content to be taking an hour or so off with her fiancé.

They crossed the Arno and sped through the city suburbs. It was already oppressively hot. Joanne searched in her bag for a tissue to wipe sticky palms. Florence always seemed more suffocating than anywhere else.

Now they were climbing, leaving behind the city streets; soon they'd have some air . . .

"*Mein Gott!*" Hans exclaimed and the car swerved.

Joanne was jerked forward, sharply, against her seat-belt as he braked. A Fiat had shot from a turning to their left and she knew even Hans's swift reaction would fail to avert a collision. In the split-second before the inevitable impact, she thought the crash couldn't have been more certain to happen if it had been intentional.

The dreadful scraping of metal against metal seemed to continue endlessly as the other car tore into theirs. Joanne heard a scream and then recognized it as her own as the glass in the driver's door shattered and its panelling buckled, thrusting Hans hard against the steering wheel. Again, she screamed, as she watched his face twist in agony.

And still the Fiat tore into their car, forcing in the side of the long bonnet, dashing out their headlamps, until its driver cut across their path and accelerated away.

"Hans!" Joanne wrestled to free herself from her seat-belt so she could assist him. His eyes closed, he was biting his lip against the pain. Vainly, she struggled to ease him away but he was trapped between the battered door and the steering column.

And it was up to her; there was nobody else in sight. She'd longed to be away from the hot city, now she longed with all her heart to be able to summon help. She wasted further precious seconds scrabbling with now-bleeding fingers at the wreckage before leaping from the car and running round to the other side. The rest was easier—Hans's door was wrenched off its hinges. She only had to pull and it came away.

As the pressure eased, he let out an enormous sigh, leaning his head against the steering wheel. "Thanks," he murmured, hoarsely, "I will be all right in a minute."

Joanne helped slide back his seat, giving him the chance to take in more air. She got in beside him. "Let's have a look . . ." She loosened off his shirt, gently felt his ribs. He winced, but at least he didn't cry out with pain. And she could detect no irregularity; with luck he was only severely bruised.

"Phew!" Hans exclaimed presently, shaking his head in an attempt to clear it. "That was close!"

"Too bloody close!" Joanne agreed, then

started refastening his shirt. "Though I don't think your ribs have cracked. I'll be happier when we've got you to the nearest doctor."

"No," Hans protested, "that is not necessary."

"Of course it is. You could have internal injuries, or I might be wrong about your ribs. Then there's the shock . . ."

"I have told you," he said, firmly. "No! We will return to Florence, there is no time now to continue to Fiesole. Even if this car were capable of making the trip."

She assisted him out on to the road and together they inspected the damage. As well as the ruined door, scrape marks were gouged the length of the driver's side, culminating in the mass of twisted metal ramming the front wheel. As they watched, the tyre subsided.

"M'm," Hans remarked, ruefully, as the first motorist they'd seen since the accident slowed beside them. Taking in their situation at a glance, he offered them a lift into Florence.

All the way back, Joanne was eyeing Hans worriedly, but although he occasionally flinched his colour was slowly returning. Their rescuer offered to drive them to the hospital, but Hans thanked him with a smile and declined the offer. "I will get a cab there from the hotel."

Joanne sighed; if only she believed him!

She tried again to talk him round when they reached their hotel.

"Please do not argue, Joanne, I am perfectly fit," he persisted, and hurried ahead of her into the foyer.

Elena, emerging from the dining-room, stood motionless and let out a clearly audible gasp when she saw him. "Hans!"

He tried to laugh. "Sorry—I cannot make it to your friends'—had a bit of a smash."

Catching up with him, Joanne had her attention riveted by Elena's expression. She was gaping at Hans, as though she had seen a ghost.

9

WITH the help of hotel staff, Joanne marshalled her tourists, complete with baggage, into the coach. She'd sent Hans to lie down for the half-hour remaining before they must depart, and had left a bemused Elena standing near Reception.

When Hans reappeared she was relieved to see he looked somewhat better, although she gathered he'd spent some time on the telephone reporting the accident, and arranging to have the Mercedes removed from the scene.

"It'll be a long job, putting that to rights," he remarked. "Still—could have been worse . . ."

"Much worse!"

"I got quite a shock when I looked in the mirror upstairs. No wonder Elena reacted as she did!"

"You still don't look up to driving this coach."

"Hey now—who is the boss around here? I am taking this vehicle to Thun, and that is final."

"Just make sure it isn't! Final for you, I mean. There've been too many incidents recently."

"I agree. And have given details to the *Polizia*. Let us leave everything to them, eh?"

"I only want you alive and well—it's looking as though you won't even last until our wedding!"

Hans made a rude noise and began singing to himself, off-key, effectively ending the conversation.

When they stopped for a break, he led Joanne aside. "*Liebchen*—stop looking so worried. I am fine—and you've got your way, now I've contacted the *Polizia*."

"Hans, do you believe the crash was an accident?"

"I am damned sure it wasn't! That Fiat came straight out of a side turning and rammed us. I saw his eyes, seconds before the impact—his only emotion was determination. And he didn't hesitate afterwards—as one would after a genuine accident!"

"Oh, Hans—they'll get you, they will . . ."

"Don't be hysterical!" he snapped, then squeezed her shoulders. "I know, Jo—how you must be feeling. But your anxiety I do not need. I have got to keep my head, that is the only way we will defeat them."

Joanne felt inadequate to persuade him to take precautions against further mishap—a task commensurate with restraining the tide from turning. But, she reassured herself, they'd be together for the next few days. And they were nearing the end of the season.

Re-boarding the coach, Joanne remembered something. "I wonder how Elena has coped—with young Kurt. Though I couldn't see why she was incapable of dealing with her own son anyway. Some mother!"

She saw Hans smile to himself and changed the subject before he made some comment on her disapproval of his sister-in-law.

*　　*　　*

Accustomed to the routine at their hotel near Thun, they soon had everything organized and, with the proprietor's blessing, were off in a hired car.

Hans seemed fully recovered from the morning's incident.

On arriving at the chalet, he led her round the side to the garage. Inside was a navy Lancia Beta, again bearing the Company insignia. Hans walked all round, examining it, feeling the tyres. "I must get that checked over—we shall need it now for the honeymoon. They will be months repairing the Merc."

Frau Lindt opened the front door to them moments later, and embraced them in turn. "See," she exclaimed. "I was determined to show you how well I am today. But come in . . . now it is autumn the nights are cool up here . . ."

Joanne was surprised, after being introduced to the twenty or so people already arrived, to see Elena chatting in one corner and Kurt standing nearby. She made her way across to Elena determined to ease their somewhat awkward relationship, if only to please Hans. "You and Kurt seem the best of friends now," she remarked, warmly—hoping that was so, for Kurt was showing his normal lack of interest in his mother.

Elena hesitated momentarily. When she spoke it was in English; maybe that had delayed her response. "Oh—yes. I was foolish to trouble Hans, was I not? My son needs only his mother—one day's absence convinced him of that."

The outer door seemed to open incessantly

during that first hour admitting more guests until Joanne estimated something like fifty must be present.

"Forty," Hans corrected her, "large though it is the chalet will not take more. But I gather Mother is so elated about our engagement that she cannot do enough to show her delight."

Mathilde had laid on a fondue which, Joanne discovered, as well as being delicious, proved fun. It was also extremely filling—especially since Joanne had to try each garnish and returned repeatedly to her favourite black cherries which were smothered in thick cream.

When Hans eventually led her towards the large entrance hall where a four-piece group had assembled for dancing, she was afraid she would be too full to be energetic. But he laughed away her protestations and swept her into his arms, to whirl her round the room.

She looked forward to dancing away the hours with her fiancé but there were further introductions to be made and courtesy dances to take them from each other, so it was midnight before Hans took her once more into his arms. The dance was a foxtrot and as he held her close Joanne reflected on how much had happened in the short time since he'd first partnered her in the night-club in Rome.

As the last notes died away, Hans took her to his study. Entering, he fingered his tender ribs, smiling away her anxiety.

"I have much to say to you tonight," he began, closing the door behind them, "and I am scared there will be no time. We have already been engaged for some while and I have not found an opportunity to talk in detail of our future."

He indicated a chair, but once Joanne was seated he remained standing, looking down at her. "I . . . intend that we shall buy a small chalet—not far away. I have several possibilities in mind."

"But—I thought . . ."

". . . we would live here? Naturally, Mother would be pleased. The place is big enough to avoid our being crowded. I know, however, that you are not over-fond of Elena—nor, for that matter, am I. But this is her home. We cannot turn her out—and I am attached to young Kurt."

"So why not . . ."

"Would you be happy in this situation?"

"I'd try."

Hans smiled, drawing her to her feet and

pulling her to him. "I believe you would—for my sake. But, Joanne, those initial months of marriage will be vital. Nothing will be allowed to spoil them." He paused. "I know Elena—she is attractive, but has overlooked attractive behaviour. So, my Jo, we will have our own small place—if, one day, things alter and we can happily make our home here, then we will do so."

"You mean if Elena remarries?"

"Why not?" Hans chuckled suddenly. "She has the figure to delight any man!"

His choice of phrase was unfortunate. Instead of being reassured by these plans for their future, Joanne was disturbed, and she couldn't show it. Why had Hans, twice, commented on Elena's pleasing appearance?

*　　*　　*

Although she slept, it must have been restlessly, for Joanne was exhausted when her travel alarm shrilled her awake. After a hasty shower she felt more human, however, and could smile at last night's jealousy. She *knew* Hans, didn't she? She was the one he loved, and he it was who'd suggested living away from the Lindt chalet.

233

She was singing to herself as she folded and packed her evening gown and threw overnight things into her bag before going down to breakfast.

Frau Lindt was alone, heading the table, her face drawn and pale but smiling nevertheless. "I decided I would do this right—taking breakfast with you and Hans before you leave."

"That's sweet of you, but please don't overtax yourself . . ."

Frau Lindt chuckled. "I shall not—the moment you two have left I shall sneak back to bed!" She hesitated, then went on. "I am glad we are alone—I wanted to talk to you, without Hans. He tells me you are having your own home—a wise decision. Oh, I won't pretend I wouldn't have loved having you here, but I know you won't neglect me. Hans has been a son in a million, flying back home from all over while I have been ill. And you, dear Joanne, already I think of you as the daughter I was never granted . . ."

Joanne smiled, her eyes brimming suddenly.

"But I am digressing," her hostess continued, "and Hans will be with us any minute. I want you to know, my dear, that

234

the chalet will belong to Hans and yourself one day. I have made a new will—everything is settled. I have arranged that a small house be built, as soon as possible, in the grounds—for Elena and Kurt."

"Oh, but I wouldn't want that. It seems so unkind."

"Unkind!" Frau Lindt cried. "You do not know what she has done to this family." Her eyes filled with icy rage, all the more dangerous because it was cool, controlled. "From the moment I met her, Elena made me hate her. Yes—*hate*. Once she saw this place she was determined to live here. I have . . . tolerated her, but Klaus has been gone for a long time now. Whatever courtesy or charity I show is for the child's sake. So, *Liebchen*, do not expect me to be overkind to her!" Closing the subject, Frau Lindt glanced at the clock. "Hans is late. I asked Mathilde to call him; I was awake early but heard no sound from his room. I heard how you reproved him once for being late!" She winked, suddenly mischievous. "Keep him on his toes, Joanne!"

Mathilde came in then, frowning. "Herr Hans is not there, Madame."

"Not . . . there?"

Together, Joanne and Frau Lindt rose.

235

Mathilde stood there, helplessly shaking her head.

"I'll go and see . . ." Joanne said, quickly, hustling the housekeeper towards the stairs.

"His bed has been slept in, Miss Joanne, but it is quite cold—I felt the sheets. I believe he has been away since the early hours."

"He's probably still in the bathroom."

"Herr Hans uses the one next to his room and it's open, see . . ."

"Perhaps he's in the garden."

"In the rain?"

Looking across, Joanne saw torrents coursing down the window.

"Well, *I* don't know . . . You must have some idea where he'd go, Mathilde; you've known him for years."

"And he would never go anywhere without he had his coffee and roll. Always before going out, even as a child, he would eat something."

Joanne sighed, consulting her watch. "If Hans doesn't appear soon I'll have to leave without him. We can't both vanish!" She was fast becoming impatient—it was bad enough having to contemplate work after last night's party, without this added complication—and anxiety.

"Maybe he couldn't sleep. He made him-self breakfast and . . ." Joanne remembered something ". . . and decided to take a look at the Lancia. He said it needed checking."

She dashed downstairs, snatched the garage key from the hook indicated by Mathilde and ran through the downpour.

Fumbling a little in her agitation, Joanne unlocked the garage.

The Lancia was there no longer.

"I don't understand," Frau Lindt exclaimed when Joanne told her. "Hans would not go off without you, like this . . . with no word. And leaving the hire car."

Joanne looked at the Volkswagen in which they'd arrived. "At least I can get back to the hotel—if I drive myself there, and it seems I'll have to! Wait till I find Hans! I didn't know he was addicted to practical jokes—what's more, I see no humour in this! I've worried enough about him recently . . ." Recalling that Frau Lindt knew nothing of yesterday's accident, nor presumably of the mishap with the coach, she let her voice trail off.

"I'm sorry," she then began, "but I'll have to be off—I've never driven this type of car, never driven on your mountain passes—nor, for that matter, on the right hand side."

"Joanne," Frau Lindt protested, "you must not attempt it—you will kill yourself."

"I won't, I'll be careful."

"No, listen—I will call Elena, she will drive you. She is a competent driver."

"I couldn't trouble her . . ."

"I insist." Hans's mother was already at the staircase where Mathilde remained motionless. After a murmured conversation the housekeeper started up the stairs.

Joanne turned away, deciding to save time by putting her bag in the car.

Moments later, Frau Lindt, her face expressionless, came out on to the steps. "Elena is not in her room." She sounded shattered.

Joanne felt torn between longing to comfort this frail lady, suddenly reduced to bewilderment, and the knowledge that she must return to the hotel to ensure her tourists reached the airport. She sighed helplessly and took Frau Lindt gently by the shoulders. "You're not to worry, there will be some perfectly ordinary explanation, you'll see. Mathilde will contact the police, in due course, if nothing is heard. But I'm sure there'll be some news—soon. I'll phone from the airport, if I don't get the chance before then."

Hans's mother nodded, numbly.

"I'm sorry," Joanne went on, "but I must go."

"Of course." The older woman breathed deeply, straightened her fragile figure. "For the sake of the Company."

She drew Joanne to her for a brief, earnest embrace. "Take care, *Liebchen*."

Joanne hurried towards the car then; before she decided to stay.

Descending the mountain, she refused to think of anything but handling the unfamiliar vehicle. Driving through the streets, she tried to dismiss the irrational hope that Hans would be at the hotel when she arrived.

He wasn't.

With fifteen minutes to departure, their clients were assembling near Reception. The proprietor had organized his staff into collecting baggage at one end near the door. The surprise on their faces when she came in alone told her there'd been no message from Hans.

Joanne's heart started pounding irregularly. Her mouth dry, she swallowed hard on the lump rising to her throat in panic. She took a deep breath and crossed to the desk. "I suppose . . . there's been no word from Hans?"

"No. Is he not with you?"

She shook her head and hurried towards the telephone.

The office told her they'd send a relief driver, but he couldn't be there for half an hour. She thanked them and hung up. She could do nothing except ensure that the baggage was beside the coach for loading when the driver arrived with a spare set of keys.

Waiting around was dreadful. If only they could be on their way she'd be occupied, concentrating on seeing everything went smoothly. But here she had to force her mind away from the unexplained disappearance of her fiancé. And yet when the replacement driver arrived Joanne would have preferred to remain where she was, in case Hans turned up. There was no room for her preferences, however, she had a job to do—and one which would leave her no chance to follow up any ideas as to where Hans might be. Not, she thought ruefully, that she was likely to have any such ideas!

Hans's disappearance couldn't have been more complete if he'd intended to baffle her.

And had he, she wondered as soon as everyone was settled into the coach. She couldn't dismiss last night's conversation in his study. Everything Hans had said about their future had been spoiled for her. Because twice—briefly perhaps, but *twice*—he'd mentioned Elena's attractiveness. Now Joanne couldn't escape this fear that Hans might, at last, have found Elena irresistible.

Repeatedly, she tried disciplining her attention towards occupying her tourists during these last few hours of their holiday. She took them into Lucerne where some of them made straight for the lake, others for the shops. And so she was alone again, attempting still to understand. For Hans had declared his love for her—had demonstrated only last evening his wish to marry her. She must trust him. There would be a reason—there *had* to be—for his vanishing with Elena.

She had read in his eyes the yearning for her understanding. And she'd known that it was as right for Hans as for herself that there should be this . . . sharing.

Bewildered, miserable, Joanne wandered beside the lake. Suddenly she noticed a telephone kiosk and hurried across to ring the Lindt chalet.

Mathilde answered, with the information that her mistress, distressed, had been ordered to bed.

"And any news of Hans, Mathilde—or of Elena?"

"I am sorry, Miss Joanne, we have heard nothing. Perhaps you could phone again, later . . ."

"Of course, from our hotel this evening." Joanne remembered Hans's nephew. "Is Kurt dreadfully upset by his mother's absence?"

"About her—no. But then, though I should not say this, he has little real affection for her. No, Kurt is deep in uncharacteristic sulks, because his Uncle Hans could leave without saying goodbye."

Restlessly, Joanne returned to wandering by the lake. She was staring at the ground, oblivious to her surroundings, when a car sped towards her. Something about the manner in which it was being driven forced her to look.

The driver wore a white safari suit, reminding her of Neville.

If only it were—he'd be able to offer advice, or, at least, would provide a respite from her lonely anxiety.

Joanne turned as the car passed and saw it was stopping. The driver parked, then got out—and she recognized Neville.

"Joanne!" he exclaimed, a hand outstretched for hers as he came towards her.

"Oh, Neville, I am pleased to see you!" she responded, and watched him smile.

He retained her hand, leading her to a nearby bench. "What is it, my dear? Nothing wrong, I hope."

"Please help me," she begged emotionally. "Hans has disappeared—I've got to find him."

Neville didn't even express astonishment; she wondered if he'd not understood.

"I've got to find him," she reiterated. "His mother's ill—this anxiety could finish her. And . . ." her voice faltered, and she controlled it, ". . . Elena's gone as well."

"Say something can't you!" she exclaimed when he didn't speak. "I've been waiting and waiting to tell somebody, and now you . . ."

But tears had won, she could say no more.

"Look, honey," Neville began, facing her. "I'm in an awkward position—you know how I feel about you . . . and *I* know how you feel concerning Hans! When did he go missing?"

243

"Some time between 3.00 a.m. and break-fast."

"Today? I think your panic is somewhat premature."

He was entwining his fingers with hers: "Don't you remember, Joanne, what I said earlier? Or have you preferred to dismiss my warning?"

Questioningly, Joanne looked into his face. He seemed genuinely concerned.

"I mentioned, didn't I, the gossip sur-rounding Hans and his relationship with his sister-in-law. I tried to put you off—okay, partly because I hoped to get a look in if your eyes were opened. But also because—" he seemed to swallow, then continued, "—be-cause I care too much to see you hurt."

Embarrassed now, because her thoughts could only be of Hans, she attempted to with-draw her hand, but Neville only tightened his grip.

"So—you want help?" He smiled. "I'll do all I can—you know that. And don't forget I have contacts throughout Europe."

"You're a real friend, Neville—I'll never forget this."

"Well . . . where do we start?"

"I don't know—I hoped you might have some suggestion."

"Did he vanish from your hotel?"

"No—we were at their family chalet, in the mountains. There was a party last night—to . . . to celebrate our engagement."

"Poor love!" Neville squeezed her hand. Again, Joanne checked her instinctive recoil. He was being kind, and he was going to help; she'd have to lower her defences against anyone who wasn't Hans. If only as far as not flinching from Neville.

"Have you reported him missing?"

"I haven't—it was much too soon when I left the chalet; but they will, from there, if he doesn't turn up." After a pause, she went on. "I rang them just now, but there's no news."

"It may be some time before there is any—you understand that? It could be weeks, Joanne, if he and Elena . . ."

"He *wouldn't*!" Joanne asserted, vehemently. "He would not go off with her. I *know* Hans."

"Do you? How well—and for how long?" Neville demanded.

Then he noticed her expression. "Okay, okay. Let's suppose then he'd some reason for going off, *disappearing*, without even telling his sick mother, where would he go?"

"I don't know," Joanne confessed, miserably. Neville was making it sound much more possible that Hans had deliberately vanished with Elena.

"Precisely."

Joanne sprang to her feet, she'd had enough of this!

"Sorry, that was brutal—but I have to make you see it. Hans is still very much an unknown quantity for you, Joanne. And for the time being you can do nothing."

"Nothing?" This was what she'd feared before—alone.

"You can't go tailing him—which direction would you choose, eh?"

When she didn't answer, Neville continued, more kindly. "How long are you staying over here? When does the season finish?"

"I was staying on. We were marrying as soon as we'd stopped touring."

"Yes, but when's your last tour?"

"It's this next one—arriving today." Remembering about her clients, Joanne glanced at her watch. "And I'm meeting my people for lunch before taking them to the airport. I'll have to dash . . ."

"Then I'll push off." Neville released her hand. "Leave this with me, Joanne, I'll do what I can—ask around, someone may know something. And I'll be in touch—you're using your regular hotels?"

She nodded. "Yes—and thanks, Neville. I don't know what I'd do without you."

She stood gazing after his departing figure. Hans had misjudged Neville; the man was kind, concerned, willing to assist.

*　　*　　*

This fortnight, Joanne decided while undressing that night, *will be sheer hell.*

The afternoon and evening had seemed endless, controlling her emotions to concentrate on getting to know her clients, and on settling them into the hotel. She had also been obliged to be sociable over drinks after dinner—when all the time her heart ached because her second phone call to the chalet had brought no news. How could she maintain this—for fourteen days, if no word came to allay her anxiety? She couldn't face the prospect of one similar day, and knew that if there was no news her anguish would worsen.

She sighed; this must be done, nevertheless—she couldn't contemplate relinquishing her duty. She owed this to Hans—to the Company he cherished. Enough had gone wrong this season, she'd have to muster all her efficiency so this tour, at least, wasn't marred.

Each day she telephoned Frau Lindt, and each day felt more upset afterwards. Repeatedly, she told herself Neville was wrong—she knew Hans very well—well enough to be certain he'd never leave her for Elena.

* * *

When the coach drew up in Rome, Neville was waiting for her. Believing he had some news, Joanne's spirits soared—only to plunge when he shook his head. He insisted on taking her out during their stay in Rome and, though she could neither relax nor smile, claimed he understood. When they parted, he promised to contact her in Sorrento.

Joanne's first glimpse of the picturesque bay, with Vesuvius rising hazily beyond, brought an ache to her throat which remained with her all week. Oh, she and Hans had had their differences, agreed, but they'd been happy here simply because of being together. Now she could only rely on Neville to get her through without cracking up. And like a true friend he was available when needed, disappearing when she wanted solitude.

When the tour reached Florence Joanne had decided she must make some effort, on meeting Neville outside the *Duomo* as arranged. She consciously pretended interest while they wandered through the Straw Market, and thought she'd been quite animated—until she was leaving him to meet up with her tourists who'd spent the morning with a local guide.

"You have tried today, Joanne," Neville said, "but it doesn't matter—not with me, my dear. It'll take a long time, I know, for you to accept what's happened."

"Neville—you say that as though we can do nothing. You promised you'd help me find Hans . . ."

"I will. After all, until we locate them you'll never believe he won't return."

This implied he had an intense personal interest in sorting out her future. And she couldn't let him hope there'd ever be anything but friendship between them.

"I thought you understood. I can't let you go ahead thinking I'll change—even if I never see Hans again I'm incapable of feeling the same way about anyone else. I'm sorry . . ."

Neville tilted her chin until she met his gaze. "I know. But you will, nonetheless, need friends. I'll take the chance."

Disturbed, Joanne lay awake that night wondering if she ought to cut loose from Neville. But she knew she'd never make a loner. And he had contacts throughout Europe. Once the season ended they'd concentrate on tracing Hans. Alone, she wouldn't know where to start.

*　　*　　*

Drained by carrying on despite her heartache, Joanne turned away from waving off her last tourists at Berne airport and sought a cab to take her to Head Office—where she had to report before starting to search for Hans.

Recalling the plans he had made for introducing her around there, Joanne felt an almost physical pain as she approached the building. It was more impressive than she'd expected. Going through plate-glass doors into the marble-floored entrance, she reflected that it did indeed seem improbable that the managing director of this firm should ever have been interested in her.

She sighed dispiritedly, heading towards the department where she would sign off duty just like every other courier. Maybe it had all been a dream, or a day-dream—she knew only that the present seemed an interminable nightmare.

She gave her name to the clerk, who became instantly alert. The girl went to a near-by telephone then, after a murmured conversation, asked Joanne if she would see Herr Lindt's assistant. She agreed, readily, her heart hammering in anticipation of some development. The clerk gave her a folder and, a quick glance telling her it detailed winter sports, Joanne stuffed it into her bag. She was invited to sit and in doing so looked round at framed photographs of their fleet of coaches—and of aeroplanes. She was surprised to find the airline they used belonged to the Company.

Soon she was whisked by lift to penthouse offices and had to swallow hard, noticing

"Hans Lindt" on the door through which she was ushered. Things should have been so different . . .

"Wilhelm Schmidt," the tall, broad-shouldered man introduced himself, coming towards her, hand extended. "It is fortunate you are here today, Miss Kirkham." Hesitating only to offer a chair, he continued. "You were courier with Hans, were you not?"

"Yes, I . . . Have you heard from him?"

Herr Schmidt's expression clouded. "Not exactly . . . Er—first of all, do you know who Hans is?" When she nodded he unlocked his desk drawer and, extracting a large envelope, he withdrew a grimy piece of cloth, handing it across.

"Have you seen this before?"

"It looks like . . . it—I'm almost certain this is one of the cravats Hans wore." Her eyes misted.

Wilhelm Schmidt was nodding, his whole attitude anxious. "I was afraid so."

"Afraid? Doesn't this mean he's safe—alive? Where was this found?"

"It was mailed to us, arriving only this morning—with this . . ."

He gave Joanne a newspaper cutting,

English, which reported briefly the kidnapping of a so-far-unidentified Swiss businessman, now being kept hostage somewhere in Britain.

"There is this also . . ."

The note, typed on cheap paper, demanded a ransom of the Swiss equivalent of a million pounds—*and* the voluntary winding-up of the Company and all its subsidiaries.

"Oh, God!" Joanne exclaimed. "Now what?"

10

HERR SCHMIDT was pacing the office; he paused over by the window. "I do not know. Never have we experienced trouble of this kind."

Now he came towards her again, awkwardly, ill-at-ease. "We would like . . . No, we *must* find Hans! There is no question. Over here it would be simpler, but in Great Britain . . ." He shrugged, helplessly. "Everything over there, police methods, the press—everything is strange to us. You are English, Miss Kirkham, could you possibly assist? I know that your employment ceases with us today, but . . ."

Smiling slightly, Joanne rose. "You don't know, do you? Hans and I are going to be married. *You* want to find him—what do you think I feel! I've been . . . dead these past two weeks. You name it, Herr Schmidt, I'll do anything."

And how thankful she would be to have something constructive she might try! But all he required initially was her co-operation.

"I do not know," he continued, "whether it is best that I come to your country. Somebody must remain here lest further demands are made." He referred back to the typewritten note. "This requests the amount be paid into a numbered account in a Swiss bank—if the Company decides that is the only solution."

"They wouldn't, surely? Not when this stipulates closing the firm? When Hans was released that would break his heart!"

Nodding pensively, Herr Schmidt sighed. "But we cannot let him suffer, or worse. Hans is more than the boss—a man respected and . . . and loved by his employees . . ."

Emotion welled inside Joanne. Seeing her distress, Hans's assistant came round the desk to place a hand on her shoulder. "I am sorry, dreadfully sorry, that this has happened. Believe me, the concern of every member of the staff will be with you—and with his family, as with Hans himself wherever he might be."

"Does . . . does his mother know of this development?"

"I think not—certainly no one from here has informed her. Aware of her illness we were unsure of the wisest course. And I don't believe the Swiss press has the story yet."

"Well, I think she should be told—it'll be worrying but she'll know that when this was written Hans was still alive."

He agreed. "Shall I break the news to her?"

"Let me; she is, after all, my future mother-in-law."

Wilhelm Schmidt seemed relieved.

"Is there anything else?" Joanne asked.

"Only to beg you to keep in touch. When do you return to England?"

"Tomorrow, providing I reach the Lindt chalet tonight."

"I'll lay on a car."

"It's all right, thanks."

"Miss Kirkham, you are my boss's fiancée, and are under great stress. Surely you can allow us to smooth your path?" He raised the receiver of an internal phone, dialled, then requested a car to be sent to the main entrance.

"Will you stay the night with Frau Lindt?"

"I imagine she'll invite me."

"Then tell the driver to take you to the airport tomorrow. I am putting the man at your disposal whilst you are in our country—use him!"

"Thank you very much." Joanne prepared to leave.

"I only wish we could do more. Wait a minute—take the driver with you to England—you need some assistance."

Remembering Neville, Joanne shook her head. "Thank you but I have a friend who's going to help. I'll let you know, though, if we need further assistance. And when I've contacted the police I'll give you a buzz."

Herr Schmidt began scribbling and handed her a scrap of paper. "This is my home number—do not hesitate to call any time, day or night; you have this number, here?"

Joanne nodded then watched, puzzled, as he produced a wad of travellers' cheques.

"No one knows what expense you may incur—use these."

"But I . . ."

His lips twitched. "Miss Kirkham, I am surprised you are engaged to anybody as masterful as Hans Lindt! You seem very independent." Before Joanne could respond, he grinned. "I like you for that."

He shook her warmly by the hand and escorted her to the door. "Take every precaution, we cannot know how dangerous is the opposition. Do not lose contact with me—and be wary of those in whom you confide."

Settling into the comfort of the waiting car, Joanne found she was enormously relieved. Maybe this was irrational, after learning Hans was detained against his will, but this was infinitely preferable to believing he'd disappeared with Elena. Now she could put her whole heart into locating him.

* * *

The Lindt chalet was uneasy with gloom. Mathilde, thinner already, said Frau Lindt was frighteningly feeble. And young Kurt was subdued; a book open on his lap, he was gazing wistfully beyond it into space.

"Joanne!" he exclaimed. "Have you seen him—have you seen Uncle Hans?"

Forlornly, she shook her head. "I only wish I had—but I have some news."

"You have? Where is he?"

"In England, they think."

"England? That's your home . . . you will find him easily."

"It's a big country, Kurt."

"No, it isn't—I have seen it, on the map. My uncle . . ." his voice faltered, then he continued, ". . . he showed me. So I could see where you live. It is an island—pink—and it is tiny."

"I know that's how it looks . . ."

"Anyway," Kurt challenged, "if that is where Uncle Hans has gone why aren't you there already—searching?"

"I'm going tomorrow—after seeing your grandmother."

"Take me with you," the boy pleaded. "Let me help."

"I can't, Kurt. And besides, you must stay here." Joanne paused, then asked the question on which so much hinged. "Has your mother returned?"

The boy shook his head. Despite her dismay, she observed that Kurt's expression registered nothing.

"Then you must remain, greet her when she returns."

"Oh, she won't come back," Kurt informed her, calmly, as though conditioned to the fact. "Whenever I was naughty she said she would leave. She has gone now."

"Kurt . . ." Joanne couldn't believe he was stating this so impassively.

"I don't care," he asserted, as if reading her thoughts. "Uncle Hans will look after me."

"*If* he survives!" Joanne found herself thinking. She pushed the idea beyond her subconscious. This was no way to begin.

Frau Lindt, supported by pillows, looked dreadful.

"Have you any news, dear?" she asked, after greeting Joanne affectionately.

"Er—yes," Joanne began. "Though I'm not sure you'll think it's good." Briefly, she related details of the ransom demand, trying to emphasize that Hans was alive when the note was sent.

"We will raise the money," Frau Lindt announced immediately. "What is money anyway—it is people who matter."

"Just a minute," Joanne interrupted. "I felt that way, too—although I couldn't help financially. But there's a further demand."

"What is it?"

"That the Company goes out of business."

Tortured, Joanne watched Frau Lindt's intense eyes reveal the conflict between a mother's desperation to save her son, and the dread that she might preserve his life only at the expense of everything for which he had worked.

Presently, Hans's mother raised her shoulders, hopelessly, and let them droop.

"They have us, have they not, *Liebchen*? We cannot win—whatever."

"There's one chance—finding Hans before . . . while he's okay."

"And where to start?"

"London, initially—the package was mailed there. According to the newspaper, our police are investigating already. They appear to have no lead, but you never know . . ." She forced a reassuring smile. "And that newspaper must be days old, there might be developments."

Before going to bed that night, Joanne rang Neville's number. The speaker, who avoided identifying himself, said Neville was in London, giving her a number there.

Joanne got through without difficulty to find Neville expecting her call. He confirmed he'd read the newspaper account.

"Did the one you saw mention Hans by name?" she asked.

There was a fractional pause and then: "Er—no, don't think so. I just assumed it was Hans."

"I'm coming to London—first possible flight tomorrow."

"Great—I'll pick you up at the air terminal."

"Aren't you working?"

"Yes—but because I spend a great deal of time travelling to meet clients, I have a good team. I can leave my manager in charge for days if necessary."

"Oh, that's fine then—thanks. Now I must get off the line, this will be costing the earth. I'll ring you when we touch down, Neville. Thanks again."

Taking leave of Frau Lindt and Kurt next morning nearly tore out her heart. The white-haired lady, fragile beyond her years, was trying too hard to be brave.

"I won't say anything facile like 'don't worry'," Joanne began, hugging her, "but try not to make yourself really ill. Hans will be dreadfully upset if you're in hospital when he returns. Now, I'll phone you as soon and as often as I can, but I'm not certain where this will take me . . . ."

Leaving Frau Lindt's room, Joanne beckoned Kurt. Closing the door behind her, she bent down to whisper: "Would you like to do something that'll please your Uncle Hans?"

"Of course. But how can I?"

"Your grandmother is very worried, we all are, do you understand?"

262

Kurt nodded.

"She needs you to cheer her up . . ."

He looked down, scuffing a small slippered toe against the carpet. "How?"

"By spending some time in her room when she can't get up. Maybe you could have your meals in there . . . I'll ask Mathilde. And haven't you any games—card games, or puzzles?"

"Yes . . ." Kurt seemed bewildered.

"Grandmothers love to think they're useful—couldn't you pretend you can't . . ."

". . . manage without her help?" He gave her a conspiratorial grin.

"Exactly!"

Joanne drew him close, touched his soft hair with her lips, glad Kurt wasn't too old for such affection. She left Hans's home, wondering in what state of mind she'd eventually return. Would it, please God, be rejoicing with Hans? Or, wretchedly, alone—to bring some small comfort to his distraught mother?

* * *

Neville's voice sounded welcomingly familiar when Joanne rang from the airport. And she realized she was exhausted and needed to lean on somebody.

"Wait at the terminal," he told her. "I'll come for you."

He was there when the airport bus drew in, and Joanne had to restrain her instinct to hug him—as she might an older brother. It was unfortunate Neville felt more than brotherly towards her, leaving any demonstration of her regard open to misinterpretation.

His amiable self, however, he'd soon whisked her across London and was handing over her baggage at the hotel in which she'd reserved two nights' accommodation. From there, Neville drove her to his flat near Streatham Common.

"You hungry?" he asked, when they were almost there.

Joanne was astounded to discover that, after days without appetite, she was indeed hungry.

"Yes, I am—must be coming back to England."

Neville smiled. "Want something solid, wholesome and British then?"

"I don't mind, Neville—anything'll do me, thanks."

"Right, then we'll make it Chinese, which I prefer."

He stopped in a side turning, crossed the pavement to a shop. Joanne watched him lean over the counter, consulting the menu with the yellow-skinned man in charge.

Neville was likeable enough—and attractive, she decided.

She'd noticed him that first day at Basle airport, hadn't she? Probably because he looked so right in his safari suit. But she was in love with Hans and even if the worst happened she'd consider no substitute—however attractive.

Neville emerged, got into the car, and passed her a carrier containing foil cartons from which enticing aromas wafted.

"Very handy this—I'm just round the corner. Chinese take-away places were invented for the bachelor male."

Leading Joanne into his ground-floor flat, Neville took her coat, showed her where to freshen up. When she joined him, he had the table set and was opening a bottle of wine.

Only after they'd eaten, and then on her insistence, was he diverted from reminiscences of their overseas meetings. "Sorry, Joanne," he confessed. "It's just that, seeing you again—here—I keep forgetting that this is more than a date . . ." He smiled, somewhat uncertainly she thought. "Forgive me?"

She nodded. "Now—about that ransom demand . . ."

Joanne passed on the information from Head Office—not much to go on, in all conscience, but a start.

"Didn't you mention something else in the package?" Neville asked.

"The newspaper cutting—yes. But you've seen the papers. Was it in more than one?"

"No idea—sorry. I didn't connect at first."

He seemed to make such a point of this that she threw him a curious glance. But Neville was continuing.

"No, I didn't mean that cutting, Joanne—you said something about a . . ."

"Cravat?" She was puzzled, she didn't recall telling Neville about that—had intended keeping it to herself.

"Yes," she went on, "whoever's detaining Hans sent it with the note—proof of his identity."

Suddenly Neville leaned across the table. "Joanne—you do trust me—you do know I'm trying to help?"

"I wouldn't be here otherwise. Why?"

He shrugged. "Only . . . you seemed to hesitate then. Joanne, you've got to co-operate fully if we're to succeed; you do understand?"

"Yes, but . . ."

"There's to be no holding back—you must keep me posted on every detail, on any lead the police may be following."

"You'll be in on all that, surely—visiting the police with me."

"Er—no. That's unwise—I believe I'll learn more if I keep away from them . . ." His voice dropped. "I have certain contacts, who may become uneasy if I'm seen with the law."

"Oh."

"They're great blokes—would do anything for me. But they don't go along with the cops."

"Okay. So you want *me* to liaise with the police."

"What's more natural?"

"Sure, fine."

"We can't achieve much more tonight. I suggest you call on the police tomorrow, they'll check for you on what's been done to date. I'll meet you for lunch then, well—we'll take it from there."

"If that's so, I'll get back to my hotel—I need an early night, desperately."

She refused his offer to drive her. "Call me a cab—it will serve equally well, and you need rest, also—embarking on what could prove a marathon search."

Going into the hotel, she tried to empty her over-worked mind. Tonight she must sleep. She'd had wine at Neville's and she'd have a brandy or something now. That should put her out.

★ ★ ★

The alcohol must have helped—it was five next morning when Joanne wakened. She'd have preferred sleeping longer, but this was better than for many a long night.

She was just at her door, about to go down to breakfast, when she was startled by the shrilling telephone. Neville.

He enquired how she'd slept then said he looked forward to seeing her; he'd booked a table at a near-by restaurant, would pick her up at midday.

Her visit to the police proved disappointing. They checked with somebody, presumably Scotland Yard, then confirmed the man

268

held hostage was assumed to be Hans. And that was that. They seemed, to Joanne, somewhat uninterested in his being detained.

She checked her impulse to complain. Verifying that they'd no further clue to Hans's whereabouts, she gave her hotel number, agreeing to leave everything in their hands.

She was fuming by the time Neville arrived to take her to lunch; he too seemed perturbed that they'd no further information.

"Never mind," he said, taking her coat when they reached the restaurant, "we'll find a lead somehow—if we have to pull London apart."

Later, at their corner table, he covered her hand. "Please, Joanne, don't be discouraged. Remember I'll see you through. Between us we'll find him."

She nodded, her eyes misting with grateful tears; she'd be so lost without Neville!

After lunch he told her he'd an appointment, so she was left to her own devices. Too restless to remain indoors, she began wandering . . . among lunchtime crowds, past St. Paul's, down Ludgate Hill. In Fleet Street, Joanne remembered James.

Why hadn't she thought of him earlier? He'd once refused help when Hans was all right, but now—his fate so uncertain . . . ? It was worth a try. James could only snub her—and that wouldn't affect her.

She was admitted to his office as easily as before. This time James looked up as she entered, rose, and came round his desk.

"Joanne!"

"Do you know why I'm here?" she asked, marvelling at his changed manner.

James nodded, sighed. "I'm sorry, Joanne—truly sorry."

"Did your paper run the story?"

"We were the first, then it was syndicated."

"You knew who the 'Swiss businessman' was—yet his name wasn't printed."

"Part of the deal . . . his identity wasn't revealed, initially."

"But it's revealed now?"

Silently, he passed her a copy—today's. Joanne swallowed hard, reading the headline.

RANSOM DEMAND AND CONDITIONS FOR RELEASE OF TOURIST COMPANY CHIEF HANS LINDT.

"I suppose you still refuse to say who . . ."

"Steady," James interrupted, "I'm not that

bad! I wouldn't withhold information which might speed his release. I've already cooperated with the police, only . . . there's so little to go on." He paused, then continued, sincerely. "Joanne—I know it's over between us, but I'm still concerned. I'd do anything to stop you looking so . . . haunted."

"Who gave you the story—was it the person with the gen on that missing baggage?"

"It was." He started walking towards the door.

"And . . . ?"

James glanced into the outer office, presumably to check nobody was within hearing, then closed the door and leaned against its panels. From his wallet, he extracted a photograph, passed it to her.

"Do you recognize that? He calls himself . . ."

"Neville!" Joanne exclaimed, sitting down with an involuntary suddenness. She stared from the photograph to James and back again. His expression grave, he went on, "So you do know him—I wondered. Take care, Joanne, keep away from that customer. He's in London now. Don't for Christ's sake get involved with him!"

Joanne scarcely listened to the words of warning with which James followed his bombshell; she longed only to get away—and reason things out.

He enlarged on how dangerous it might be if she encountered Neville and she agreed, hastily, to avoid him. But how could she—knowing that Neville alone might lead her to Hans? So she'd have to think—to prepare—to scheme . . .

In her hotel room, Joanne tossed her coat on to the bed, then rang for tea.

She sat at the table by the window. She must still the disbelief and fright which sent her brain scurrying fruitlessly. If she was to be any match for Neville she needed . . .

The sharp rap startled her. She stammered, "Come in . . ." Then, remembering the tea, forced a smiling thank you for the girl bringing the tray.

Her hand was shaking so much she'd to steady it to pour, and as she raised the cup and saucer they rattled.

"This won't do," Joanne said aloud, "you're not calming at all." She sipped the tea, then took slow breaths of the chill air wafting in from autumnal London.

Next she began to sort the thoughts jostling in her mind.

First, despite James's warning, she would contact Neville—he must not suspect her reluctance to have his assistance.

Somehow, she must accustom herself to spending considerable time in his company. Today's revelation convinced her this would lead, eventually, to Hans. Although the ransom demand was mailed in London he needn't, necessarily, even be in England—although Neville's presence indicated that this was the place.

Joanne was startled by the strident note of the telephone. She gazed at the instrument, alarmed; it'd be *him*—before she was prepared.

On and on it rang; she'd have to answer.

"Miss Kirkham?" She couldn't recognize the voice when she found courage to lift the receiver.

"Who . . . who is that?"

"Sergeant Rayleigh, Miss—I saw you earlier when you . . ."

"Of course—sorry, I didn't immediately recognize . . ." Joanne, relieved, flopped on to the bed.

"That's all right, Miss Kirkham. I rang

because something has cropped up . . . I'd like to discuss it—if that's convenient. I'll send a car for you, if you'll oblige . . ."

"A car? Well, all right."

"Let's say ten minutes."

Reception rang when the driver arrived. She was thankful it had been Neville's idea that she should liaise with the police. But she mustn't let him know that she suspected he was implicated in Hans's disappearance.

*   *   *

"Glad you could come," Sergeant Rayleigh began, showing Joanne into a stark interview room. "Must apologize for the surroundings, my chief has somebody with him."

He paused; Joanne sensed he was weighing her up. "Friend of yours, as a matter of fact— or so we think."

"Oh?"

"You lunched with him today," he told her, naming the restaurant.

Joanne nodded, wondering how to proceed. Surely they didn't suspect she was in league with Neville?

"I—I believed he was a friend," she started,

274

slowly. "Till today. I never doubted that he was helping me to trace Hans Lindt."

"Then what happened—today?"

"Don't you read the papers?" Joanne asked, and watched him smile.

"This?" He'd crossed to pick up a newspaper, tossing it over.

"Sergeant, I understand someone from this paper contacted you, with certain information . . ."

"Yes, though how you know that . . ." He broke off to scrutinize her.

"My . . . a friend's father owns this paper; this afternoon, I . . ."

Sergeant Rayleigh seemed amused. "Get around, don't you? I thought we'd agreed last time that you'd leave everything to us. You know, Miss Kirkham, the general public would save themselves trouble, not to mention danger, if they'd only cease to meddle!"

"Meddle! When the man I love is held captive, threatened! What would you do if your wife was abducted—leave it to the local cops?"

"Okay, you've made your point. Short of taking you into custody—and I've no reason for that—I can't control your movements.

And, as yet, we're not holding your friend in there either. So I must warn you that every moment you spend with this man . . ." He checked himself, abruptly. "Do you know who he really is, this . . . Neville?"

Joanne shook her head.

"Good—we'll keep it that way. He's well-known in certain quarters. But remember, with him your life is at risk. So keep right away. If he suspects that you know he's involved, he won't hesitate to dispose of you. He's *that* dangerous."

Here it was again—reiterating James's warning. And still she couldn't heed it. This time, too, she must conceal her intentions—and cleverly; she wouldn't readily hoodwink the police into thinking she'd quit now.

"I'm very serious . . ." Sergeant Rayleigh, hands on the table, was leaning towards her. "He'll shortly be returning to his flat; we've got to ensure that you come to no harm."

Joanne managed to smile, blandly. "I'll be only thankful to comply!" She hoped on this short acquaintance her sudden acquiescence seemed credible. "I know when I've had a narrow squeak—I want to stay alive . . ." She hesitated, a flash of inventive genius prompting her: "When you set Hans free, I plan to be around to welcome him."

"Good girl." The sergeant smiled, came over to take her by the elbow. "I knew you'd see sense. Let's face it, we are the experts."

"And," Joanne thought, on her way to her hotel, "if you fall that easily for pure fabrication, I've little confidence in the force!"

★   ★   ★

The hotel receptionist told her someone had been calling her, and gave her a number to ring. It proved to be a call box—with Neville waiting, somewhat impatiently.

"You're doing a lot of popping in and out, aren't you?" he demanded.

"How do you mean?" Joanne enquired warily.

"Keep trying to ring you—each time to be told you've just gone out."

"What do you want now you've caught me?" Immediately, she wished she'd sounded pleasanter. She was making a mess of this already.

Neville had observed her mood. "Don't take that tone with me—I'm the one trying to help, remember!"

"Sorry, Neville, sorry—I'm so up-tight. That's why I have to get out every few hours. This room's like a . . . prison. All I do is worry about Hans."

"I know—it's okay, Joanne. It won't be much longer. I've got a clue—we're off to the country, darling—soon as you can pack."

"Now?" Already—before she'd adjusted to the thought of Neville collaborating with Hans's captors. Before she worked out her next move. Before she'd found a way to lull Neville into trusting her.

"You still there?"

"Yes, Neville, of course. I was just wondering . . ."

"What?"

"If it'd be all right, with the hotel—leaving now, I mean."

"It will—had a word with Reception when I rang earlier. Settle your bill, Joanne, I'll be over to pick you up."

Whilst packing, Joanne came across the folder she'd been given at Head Office, and flung it into her case on top of everything else. As it landed an envelope slid out. Intuition made her seize it and quickly smooth out the notepaper it contained.

Joanne stared, incredulously.

Liebchen,
       (the letter began)
You will be reading this only if I have been prevented from returning to remove this letter from your Company folder. You see, dearest Jo, I would not have you more worried on my account than you are already, and so I could not speak of these things. I know, however, that any day I may set out quite normally and not come back. So I must try to tell you—and words are so inadequate—a little of what is in my heart, and some small portion of all you mean to me.

You came into my life when I was weighed down by anxieties and problems. With you, I found that I could smile still; that I wanted to smile because that might bring into your eyes the light of . . . recognition. Love grows in a moment, flourishing on unlikely ground—this you have taught me. And love gives unstintingly, and is in the outstretched hand that says "I care, I understand."

Today, I cannot forget all the times that I have upset you; for speaking sharply, for hurting you by not confiding fully, most of all for the unjustifiable doubts I've sometimes had—forgive me. There have been so many years of learning not to trust—trusting again will take some practising.

Remember this, my Joanne; only the very worst that man can do to man will keep me from your side. And if that worst should happen, remember always that in a few brief weeks you have given to me a lifetime's loving.

With all my love,
Hans.

Joanne gulped back her tears—she could spare no time for them. She was leaving, her destination unknown. First she must contact Hans's people—his mother and Wilhelm Schmidt.

As she went to the telephone she felt the warmth enveloping her. It was going to be all right now, no matter what. The letter which she'd placed in her handbag was proof indeed that Hans loved her. Nothing anyone else might say or do could alter that.

And now she had to reach Hans. She'd need all the help she could get. Herr Schmidt had offered to send someone across; she'd ask him to do so immediately.

"Thank the Lord you have phoned!" he exclaimed the moment she got through. "We

have got it, Miss Kirkham," he rushed on, "...
the vital clue. We have just received a further
ransom demand—together with Hans's wrist
watch, from somewhere called Oxenholme.
Now listen, I know the place; I changed
trains there once, visiting your lovely Lake
District ..."

"But have you told our police?" she
interrupted, urgently. And was startled by
loud knocking on the door of her room.

She shivered. There was no chance now to
ask for further help, nor to find out how
much the police had been told. If she said one
more word that mattered, Neville would
hear.

"I've got to go now," she gabbled into the
receiver and replaced it. She took a deep
breath and went to open the door.

11

NEVILLE looked immediately towards the telephone. Heart pounding, Joanne waited for him to speak. How much had he heard?

"Ringing someone? Did I interrupt?"

"Er—er, no. I'd just finished. I was calling . . . Hans's mother."

"Any more news?" he asked, over his shoulder, picking up her case.

"Not so far."

"Hard luck, darling. Never mind, we're off on the trail—something will turn up soon."

"Neville," then she stopped, aghast. She'd almost criticized his endearment. Unwise to cross him before, now it was suicidal!

"Yes . . . ?"

She followed him outside.

"Oh . . . I just wish we knew, one way or the other, whether Hans has gone off with Elena." Joanne was thinking fast. "Until I'm sure, I can't contemplate a fresh start . . ."

"And would you?" Neville persisted,

opening the car door for her. "If you learned he had—would you, Joanne?"

She gave what she hoped was a winning smile. "I . . . well, you're proving very kind—kindness, perhaps, is what endures . . ."

He waited until she was seated, slid behind the wheel and kissed her cheek. "Good!" he exclaimed.

Although she'd had no opportunity to check against a map, Joanne was positive Wilhelm Schmidt was right about where Oxenholme was. She was astonished, therefore, when Neville drove towards the M3.

About to question the direction, she checked. It was wiser to play along. Neville might have more up-to-date information; she would only learn by keeping quiet. She could fish, nevertheless, for hints. "I suppose we're tearing off like this because of that clue regarding Hans?"

Neville nodded.

"Where is he—do you know?"

"I've a good idea."

He appeared reluctant to confide, but she must find out all he knew. Besides, if she stopped quizzing him he'd be suspicious.

"Is it far?"

"Quite a distance. We shan't be there till morning."

That could make it somewhere in the West Country. Joanne frowned, thankful the darkened car concealed her expression.

Had Hans been moved since the latest ransom demand? Or was Neville whisking her away from the area where Hans was detained? If so she'd have to give him the slip, and contact the police who . . .

Oh, Lord! Did they know the latest developments? What if Head Office meant her to pass on the information . . . ?

"Please God," she prayed, "let Herr Schmidt ring Scotland Yard."

She glanced sideways at Neville, wondering if he'd stop for a break *en route*. If he did she'd get to a call box—somehow.

"You're in for a long ride," he told her presently. "May as well sleep."

Leaning back her head, she closed her eyes. This would give her opportunity to think ahead—unobserved. She must be prepared for whatever occurred.

If Neville was taking her to Hans she'd no idea what kind of show-down he planned; she must calculate how best to avoid injury to Hans or herself.

Joanne sighed; with no knowledge of their destination, contingency plans seemed virtually impossible.

Eventually, covert inspection of her watch told her that four hours had elapsed since leaving London. She stirred, feigned awakening. She yawned, stretching as far as the cramped quarters permitted.

"What time is it, Neville? I was lost to the world."

"Why?"

"I just wondered—how much longer. How far now?"

"I told you, we shan't be there for ages. Relax, can't you?"

"That's all very well—I'm famished; haven't eaten since lunch."

"Nor have I. You'll survive."

"That's what you think! Can't we stop, just for a snack?"

"Not yet, Joanne. Go back to sleep. I'll stop the car when we're nearly there and we'll stock up with food."

"I'm afraid you'll have to pull in before then—I want to spend a penny."

"Women!"

Joanne giggled. "I'm sorry." She paused, thinking. "I was saying earlier how kind you are. Don't prove me wrong, will you Neville?" She forced herself to nestle against his shoulder. "I thought we were getting on rather well."

"Okay. I'll stop, when I see somewhere that's open. Might be only a transport café."

"I don't mind." So long as it has a public phone!

At last Joanne sat upright, eagerly, spotting the lights of a wayside café.

As she left the car she looked round hopefully for a telephone, saw a familiar kiosk to the right of the building. Unfortunately, the "ladies" was in the opposite direction.

"Aren't you going in?" Neville demanded.

"Later—think I'll have something to eat first; if I leave that till just before we set off, I shouldn't have to ask you to stop again."

Joanne followed him inside and up to the long counter. The place was dingy and none too clean, with oil-cloth-covered tables. "Not quite us, is it? But it will serve—admirably."

Joanne watched despairingly as three men ahead of them chose the only table away from the windows. Would Neville see her approach the telephone?

Half-way through the curling sandwiches she rose, taking her bag. "You were right—I

286

should have gone there first. You'll have to excuse me—shan't be long."

Before Neville could comment Joanne was hurrying for the door. She turned in the direction of the toilets, certain he'd be watching. She passed the "ladies" seeking some way round behind the building to emerge on the other side.

She found a muddy path, littered with overspill from the kitchen refuse bin. Clearing her nostrils, she hurried, praying she wouldn't step in anything too obnoxious in the gloom.

Finally, she reached the far corner and discovered the kiosk was unoccupied, and hoped that vandals had left the thing alone.

"Thank God!" Joanne said aloud, finding the phone intact. She wasted no time before dialling.

They seemed an age connecting her with Sergeant Rayleigh. She stood, quivering, every nerve alert for a sign of Neville coming out to the car.

At last the sergeant answered. "Can't take long over this," she gabbled, after identifying herself. "Has our Swiss office contacted you?"

"Not for a couple of days."

"Oh. Well, they've received another ransom demand—postmarked *Oxenholme*. I'm . . ." Joanne stopped, remembering Sergeant Rayleigh's warning. ". . . I'm trying hard *not* to follow that up. Can *you* . . . ?"

"Right away. We'll organize a search of every building in the area. Don't worry—we'll find him yet . . ."

"Thanks. I've got to go now."

Joanne closed the heavy door, carefully, silently, and returned the revolting way she'd come.

"You've been long enough," Neville remarked, which threw her—she thought she'd been quick.

"That was a somewhat intimate comment!"

He laughed. "Sorry—keep forgetting we're not . . . that close—yet."

Joanne made herself match his mood. "Oh, well . . . you never know."

Back in the car, he turned to her. "You seem . . . different, Joanne, not so . . ."

Heart thudding apprehensively, she waited.

". . . not so wary," Neville finished.

"If only you knew!" she thought, thanking her stars she'd apparently mustered some acting ability. But how on earth would she keep this up?

"Come on," she urged. "The sooner we get there, the sooner we'll know how things stand."

Neville leaned towards her. Joanne braced herself for the inevitable kiss—which landed full on her lips.

She remained tense afterwards, her mind further troubled with holding off Neville without offending him. The last thing she needed was a row. Whatever the cost he must suspect nothing.

Whatever the cost?

* * *

Through half-closed lids, Joanne watched the day break—judged from the scenery they were crossing Dartmoor or Exmoor—didn't fancy either in isolation with the man beside her. Perhaps . . . she experienced again the unreasoning hope that Hans might have been moved and that she was *en route* to his hideout. Even being detained herself was preferable to incarceration with Neville amid this . . . wilderness.

This kind of spot would be acceptable to

Hans's captors. A man could be concealed here for weeks without arousing suspicions. She shivered. She ought to have told the police where she was heading—and risked their annoyance for disregarding their admonition.

Without warning, Neville drew into the yard of a stone-built farmhouse. Though the buildings appeared deserted, he went unhesitatingly to the front door. He held a key which—inexplicably—he didn't use. Instead he called through the letter-box. "Max, it's me—Neville. Open up, will you?" He turned to Joanne. "They think I'm in on the kidnap plot. It was the only way to . . ." He broke off, looking puzzled. "Strange . . . no answer." Again he bent to the letter-box. "Waken up, Max—I've got the girl."

Nothing happened. The only sound was the wind howling round the farm.

Neville shrugged and looked at the key he held. "Oh, well . . . take care, darling—they may shoot if they don't realize it's us. Keep behind me—don't make any sudden movement."

He eased the door open a fraction, then wider, and walked soft-footed into the house. Early morning light revealed that the place was tidy—too tidy for anywhere inhabited. Neville ushered her inside then went from room to room calling Max—whoever *he* was. She let him go upstairs alone, convinced now that the farm was deserted.

He came downstairs, crumpling paper into his pocket. "They've left a note. Had to move on—somebody was getting inquisitive."

Joanne turned. "Right then—let's get after them . . ." She was testing his reaction, she'd sensed that this place hadn't been occupied recently. Neville was acting some scene.

He was quick. Before she reached the door his hand was on its handle. His back was against the solid oak.

"No! We . . . can't. They're sending someone for us. I don't know the way."

"I see." She had to appear convinced. If it'd been warmer, she'd have removed her coat . . . to show she intended stopping. But she was shivering in the damp chill of the empty house.

"Could we light a fire?"

"Good idea—later. First though . . ." Neville glanced to the stairs. "There's a bed. Truth is, I'm flaked out after driving through the night. Shall we . . . ?"

His hand extended towards her, he was

waiting. And she couldn't think of a response. Because if she refused he might turn nasty, certainly he'd no longer accept her pretended change of attitude. Too much hung on Neville trusting her.

Joanne placed her hand in his.

At the staircase she stopped. She could assume some modesty. "Neville, I . . . er . . ."

"Only to sleep," he said, "*if* you insist."

Inside the bedroom he took her by the shoulders. "I'd never force anything on you, darling—knowing how you feel still about that fellow . . ."

"Thanks."

Joanne noticed the bed wasn't made up. "There are no sheets, blankets . . ."

Neville went straight to a built-in cupboard.

"He's no stranger to this place!" Joanne thought as he tossed bed linen on to the bed. Another shiver ran through her—of apprehension. Supposing this was Neville's house, supposing nobody came—ever. She'd know then his story was a fabrication and that *she* was the intended victim—or worse.

She must keep her head. Maybe lying down would serve her well. She'd have the chance to evolve some plan. If Neville slept she could steal downstairs, find a telephone.

Joanne yawned as they made up the bed. "You must be right, I need rest as well."

She didn't intend undressing, but Neville wasted no time stripping to his underwear. Stacking loose change and two key rings on the table, he got into bed.

"Won't that get crushed?" he demanded, staring at her dress.

"Doesn't matter."

"Oh, come on . . . ! Joanne, you can't be that innocent. Don't you trust me at all?"

She swallowed a sigh. She dared not admit that she'd no faith whatsoever in him.

Resisting the inclination to turn her back, Joanne removed her dress. Now she'd have to brave getting into bed beside Neville who was facing the spot where she would lie. She must concentrate solely on his leading her to Hans.

The sheets icy, Joanne shuddered, then lowered her eyelids against the curious gaze too near her face.

"You're cold . . ." His arm came round her. "Let's warm you . . ."

"I'm all right."

Neville laughed, quietly, fluttering her

hair. "Never let it be said I let my women shiver!"

Frantically, Joanne blotted out another wave of aversion. She must exercise her weary brain. There had to be an escape somehow. She couldn't remain here, with this man. But if she left . . . ? What chance had she of finding Hans? Ever? Neville would be after her immediately, would detain her, overpowering her if necessary.

"You are tense," he murmured. "Let go, Joanne—I'll look after you. We'll both feel better after some kip. Then we'll be off after Hans."

Suddenly she thought of something. "We won't hear when they come for us—if we're both asleep. I'll wait downstairs . . ."

Neville's arms tightened round her. "There's no need, Joanne—there is a perfectly good bell."

She held herself rigid, hoping Neville's long drive really had tired him—sufficiently to accelerate sleep. Because if he slept she might manage to . . .

She couldn't concentrate on plans, because with one arm around her still Neville had moved the other hand, to her breast. "What were you saying, Joanne, earlier—if Hans is

294

with Elena . . ." Instantly, she was alert: what was she letting herself in for?

"Neville," she began, "if these people are holding Hans Lindt, how can you suppose he's still with her?"

"Didn't I tell you? They apprehended them both—together."

Joanne didn't believe him, didn't *want* to believe him, but he'd surely defeated her argument!

"Sorry, dear, I thought you understood that." His lips were against her hair, his fingers were straying down from her breast.

"No!" Joanne said, firmly. "There must be some mistake. And if there isn't . . . Neville, can't you see—you don't just stop loving somebody—can't immediately be turned on by someone else." Wouldn't that stop him?

Neville took away his hand. "Am I so repulsive?"

When she didn't reply he took that as the answer he sought and started caressing her cheek. Joanne wanted to scream but *for whom*, for heaven's sake? Here, nobody would hear her.

How could she escape? If she tried anything Neville would beat her to the door. He wasn't slow.

In any way.

Although she'd edged her face along the pillow away from his hand, she was still clasped unwillingly against his body. And she recognized what this was doing to him.

His breathing was quickening, hot against her neck. If it came to a tussle she'd no hope. What could she do? Pretend to meet him halfway, lull him into a false sense of security? She could make her mind a blank, maybe; think of Hans alone—held captive, miles away . . .

Neville's lips claimed hers, fiercely, and Joanne forced herself not to withdraw.

"That's better," he whispered. "Don't expect me to be that subnormal! I've wanted you for months, Joanne, you know how I've pursued you."

She had to still her derisive response. Any pursual had been for his evil intent and no other reason.

"Just let me hold you," he went on, persuasively, "know you are near . . ."

Again, she tried to focus her mind on Hans—in some beleaguered house. Its isolation as complete as this perhaps . . . ? Or was he in an anonymous street where nobody knew their neighbours?

Thinking of Hans was effective in that she no longer feared Neville, saw instead a ridiculous vulnerability in his pulsations—a vulnerability, nevertheless, which would never win *her* sympathy.

She lost all sense of time as she lay there, waiting for him to quieten, then gave a great sigh of relief as at long last he seemed to relax. He released her, almost abruptly, and turned away from her.

Ears straining, Joanne listened. Presently, she was rewarded with the sound of Neville's measured breathing—confirmation that he slept. She, also, could relax.

She timed fifteen minutes, cautiously put one foot to the floor, then the other. Neville remained asleep, even emitted the occasional muffled snore. Joanne snatched the car keys, stuffing them into her bag, then crept, barefoot, down the stairs.

She found the telephone in the kitchen. She must ring through to Wilhelm Schmidt, learn if he'd heard anything of Hans being moved. Then she would phone the police.

Joanne lifted the receiver, started to dial. It was then she noticed the absence of a dialling tone. She replaced the receiver, waited, raised the thing again. Nothing!

Tears welled inside her. She stared, disbelievingly, at the useless instrument in her hand.

"It's disconnected." Neville's voice, immediately behind her, made her start.

Joanne swung round. For at least a minute they measured each other with wary eyes.

She forced a smile. "You made me jump! I was phoning Frau Lindt—to find out how she was and to ask if . . ."

". . . if she'd heard anything. Do you ring her daily?"

"Usually. She is ill, frantic with anxiety."

Neville was nodding. "Well—sorry, but there's nothing you can do from here."

It struck Joanne that he'd known the phone wasn't working—establishing that he was familiar with this house, as she'd supposed. Again, she could only play along. For the moment . . .

"Sorry I disturbed you," she said. "Go back to bed."

He shook his head. Did this mean he intended remaining alert now, lest she give him the slip? Joanne assumed an amiable expression, there was no sense in advertising her mistrust.

"Aren't you tired now?" she asked.

"No."

She went to the stairs. "I'll get my dress . . ."

Neville followed her. "Yes, it is somewhat chilly. I'll find some logs next . . ."

Joanne removed the rest of her clothes from the bedroom, left Neville dressing. She called back up the stairs: "Would you like coffee, or tea or something, dear?"—stressing the endearment, for his reassurance. "And I'll see if there's any food . . ."

"You're a brick, Joanne," Neville exclaimed, coming downstairs again. "Most girls would panic, isolated with a strange man . . ."

"Hardly strange!"

Her words brought a smile to his lips, as she'd hoped, then Neville kissed her, quickly.

"I'd be more content though," Joanne persisted, "if you'd light a fire!"

Neville laughed. "Let that be a warning to me—you could become a nagging woman!" And he went, whistling, through the kitchen door.

Joanne watched as he skirted the house, turned from the out-buildings towards the garden. It was sloping and had a wooden shed at the top. Neville retrieved a key, *again* unhesitatingly, from beneath its eaves, unlocked the door and vanished from sight.

Joanne fled. Seizing coat and bag, she flung herself towards the front door. Abruptly, she came to a halt. A door to her left stood ajar—through it was a small room, crammed with suitcases *and each one still bore a very familiar label!* With no time to investigate further, Joanne sped out to the car.

It unlocked at a touch and she prayed it would start as easily. She'd never liked driving a strange vehicle, today that must not matter. She'd be thankful only that Neville always chose something that could certainly move. The engine, warm still, responded immediately. She tried not to over-rev, hoping to leave without attracting his attention.

She was driving from the farm yard when he came into sight in the rear-view mirror.

Reaching the road, Joanne pressed her foot hard down. Whatever else, she must put every possible mile between herself and that man! The direction was immaterial. The looming cluster of prison buildings confirmed her guess at Dartmoor.

Reaching the A384, she turned towards Tavistock—not Exeter, the way they'd come.

That should confuse Neville when he followed; as she knew he would.

The disconnected telephone, however, would delay obtaining another car.

At Tavistock Joanne took the Launceston road, avoiding the obvious route. Later, she'd to stop near Holsworthy for petrol, but was becoming certain she'd made good her escape.

As the car ate up the miles, Joanne began to wind down. On the A388 for Bideford she allowed herself to stop for a snack. And she phoned Sergeant Rayleigh.

"Any news?" she asked immediately they were connected.

"I'm sorry—no." He sounded almost as dejected as Joanne now felt. "We've searched every building within a ten-mile radius of Oxenholme. But there's nothing."

"I see." Terribly deflated, Joanne didn't know what else to say. Her breakaway from Neville successful, she'd believed her luck was changing.

"I suppose you had the name of the place right?" the sergeant asked.

"Oxenholme, Wilhelm Schmidt said. Of course, the wretched note could have been posted there as a ruse."

301

Aware that she was going to break down, Joanne blurted: "Look, I must go." And dashed to the car.

Disappointment, coupled with her earlier fright, emerged in a deluge of tears. What was the use? she asked herself. Why go on? If the police had drawn a blank she might as well give up.

Searching vainly for a tissue in her bag, she found Hans's letter and re-read it. When she reached the end she felt ashamed of her lack of courage, and very, very determined.

While Hans lived he'd come back to her—somehow. How could she give up? If their love meant anything to her she had to keep going.

His love was all she wanted. His wealth meant nothing to her. Indeed, if the Company fell victim to these outside pressures she would be half glad. With fewer responsibilities, Hans would belong more to her. Yet would he be as happy?

Joanne sighed, and knew she'd accept whatever came—so long as Hans was there.

Still seeking a tissue, she opened the glove compartment. Something metallic was icy against her fingers. Cautiously, she took out a revolver and ammunition. She shuddered, thrusting them back. She wiped away her tears with her hand and switched on the ignition. She'd concentrate on the road instead of dwelling on the danger to which she and Hans were exposed.

Joanne had forgotten to wind her watch and for miles between Barnstaple and Lynton looked out for a clock. She was horrified when she eventually learned it was afternoon. Soon she'd have to decide between putting up for the night and driving on.

Presently rain started falling and decided for her. Exhausted, in bad driving conditions, she'd little hope of staying on the road. She'd never get to Hans if she wrecked the car. Running into Weston-super-Mare, Joanne realized this was sufficiently large to preserve her anonymity if misfortune brought Neville to the town.

She found a smallish hotel boasting out-of-season visitors. And that night she did her meal justice. She'd eaten little over the past few days. And then she caught up on some sleep, ready for another wearying day ahead of her.

* * *

303

Joanne began the day with another phone call to Sergeant Rayleigh but again it proved abortive.

It wasn't until she consulted the map in the car, that she realized she had no destination. If the police had investigated the entire vicinity of Oxenholme, there was no point in her heading in that direction.

Where then would she go?

London—the first place Neville would seek her—was out.

Feeling frighteningly alone, Joanne longed for company.

Should she go home—to her parents? Heaven knew, she'd seen little enough of them recently; until securing this courier's job, her interpreter's post had kept her in London. And she'd been a poor correspondent. But they were, nevertheless, her family and would welcome her.

Without much enthusiasm, Joanne studied the distance separating her from Ripon, began plotting a route. She sighed, dispiritedly; it seemed a long way.

Having settled her bill, Joanne left immediately—determined on reaching Ripon before nightfall. The first leg of her journey on the M5 went well and by lunch-time she'd gained the Birmingham area. After a quick meal she invested in a vacuum flask which an obliging snack-bar manageress filled with soup.

Before setting off, Joanne glanced again at the map. As she was weighing one possible route against another the name leapt from the map. Midway between Hebden Bridge and Keighley—OXENHOPE. And she knew this was the one. Postmarks were, after all, notoriously illegible.

She promised herself she'd phone the police, telling them her destination, but the first call box she came across had been vandalized. And she couldn't stop now, eager to prove she was right, and most of all to get to Hans.

It was cloudy now, though the rain had ceased. On dry roads, she accelerated hard. It was, nevertheless, late afternoon before she reached industrial West Yorkshire. Nearing Halifax, she stopped to consult the map. Unfamiliar with the locality, she must avoid going astray. She drank some soup but, anxious to press on, didn't open the sandwiches she had bought along with the soup.

Driving on again, Joanne felt excited, certain she was nearing her objective. If only she'd wondered earlier about some place similar in name to Oxenholme. How slow she'd been! But then she wasn't the only one.

The road climbed, winding out of the town, until factories and streets gave way to fields, with moors beyond. Wild, Pennine country, ominous to the lone traveller. But nothing would deter her now.

Suddenly, to the left, came a turning signposted Oxenhope. Negotiating the tight corner took two attempts. Ahead, overcast skies and lowering moors combined menacingly. Joanne switched on her headlights. Driving along, she conceived her plan to cover every road in the vicinity—investigating initially each apparently deserted building. If Hans was detained here it wouldn't be in a village street. Too many people knew their neighbours—and their neighbours' business.

She scarcely noticed the kiosk in Oxenhope and wouldn't have stopped to phone the police anyway, nor for anything else. Past the village itself, mist clung to the moors, obscuring the view all round. She turned on full beam only to have it thrown back by the mist and so adjusted the lights again.

It was several minutes before the blackened

stone building loomed through the white shroud. She slowed the car and listened after switching off the ignition. Far away a curlew called plaintively; near at hand she heard the unmistakable murmur of television and a burst of laughter. And so she pressed on. Who would provide their hostage with TV?

Twice, further along the road, Joanne stopped to listen near darkened houses, but similar domestic sounds or a parked vehicle turned her away. It was raining now and the rhythmic slap-slap of windscreen wipers increased her feeling of isolation. Alone in the middle of nowhere, Joanne shivered.

Mist swirled away revealing a cluster of lights winking atop a hill. Haworth, she judged—the hill-top community which, last century, had nurtured the uncannily gifted Brontës.

She could believe, here, that something in the very atmosphere might enslave one, fostering imagination, capturing the senses, until some creation emerged. Who would be certain the influence here was benevolent?

A sudden twist in the moorland road jerked her from her musing to swerve, fighting hard to lock round on the wheel and hold the vehicle stable. She swung from side to side of the road but regained control. Palms damp, Joanne looked down the gulley towards which she might so easily have plunged.

She was certain something moved. Halting the crawling car, she wound down her window. There it was again . . . something fluttering, white or light-coloured, and moving with the breeze. Her eyes adjusting to the gloom, she could discern a dark shape—shiny against the blot of heather. Surely this wasn't another car? Had someone else had trouble negotiating that bend? Had they fought with the steering—and failed to hold the road? But surely subsequent motorists would have seen what she was seeing. Was this road, even in daylight, rarely used?

Whatever the reason for its remaining concealed, she *had* spotted something and couldn't just drive on.

Reluctantly, resenting intrusion on time which could mean life to Hans, Joanne left the car and started scrambling among bracken and boulders below the road.

Lacking a torch, her progress was slow, but the wreck wasn't all that far away.

About seven metres from the crashed vehicle Joanne stopped, unable to go nearer.

The car, on its side, was recognizable still as a dark Lancia. Coincidence? Or the one in which Hans had disappeared . . . ? She told herself these cars were not unusual on British roads these days, but couldn't prevent the awful sinking within her.

"No—not this . . ." she whispered, aghast, to the rain-sodden air. She hadn't come this far, please God, to find him . . . dead? For what seemed an eternity, Joanne remained motionless, her eyes never straying from the car. Visions of what she might find crowded her imagination.

She glanced back to her vehicle on the road, longing to retreat. But somebody, stranger or . . . otherwise could be here, trapped, injured. She could not turn away.

In an awkward, stumbling run, slithering on the wet heathland, Joanne went forward—before she could change her mind.

Approached from this side the light, fluttering object was masked by the car. She'd have to clamber past the battered coachwork to reach . . . whatever it was. She tripped, grabbed for the car to steady herself, and touched a raised disk, some eight centimetres across. The Company insignia?

Joanne had to find out. Frantically, she

searched her pockets for the lighter she
always carried and gave it a rapid flick.
Before rain extinguished the flame she knew.
The symbol of Hans's firm was here, on this
wreckage abandoned to the desolate
Yorkshire moors.

12

JOANNE stood there, trembling. How would she ever make herself look beyond his car? She'd closed her eyes after the Company insignia had confirmed her fears, but she'd have to do something. There was no one else.

She gave herself a mental shake—what was she doing, Hans could be hurt, in pain, near death . . .

Summoning all her draining courage, Joanne continued past the car. As she suspected, the light-coloured material was a part of someone's clothing, someone with light hair who was sprawled in an awkward position, motionless. *Too* motionless. The face was turned towards the saturated heather. And she couldn't go to it.

"Hans . . ." she cried, tentatively, her voice faltering. The only sound beyond pattering rain was the mournful bleat of a sheep. Again she looked back to the road, willing somebody to come—anyone who could do what she could not. And no one did.

Shuddering, Joanne rushed to kneel beside the accident victim, igniting her lighter before cowardice drove her away. She made herself touch the head, turning the face towards her. Caked with blood, flesh torn away over the dead, staring, eyes was . . . Elena.

Relieved though she was that this corpse wasn't Hans, Joanne was badly shaken—and thankful that her lighter revealed no more of this mess that had once been human. Gently, she took the flimsy scarf from around Elena's neck, placing it over her face.

And then, galvanized into action, she returned to the Lancia, flashing her lighter up and down, from side to side—checking and re-checking that Hans was not trapped inside. The car was empty.

Now she ran, this way and that, over tussocks of heather, tough bracken ripping her tights, her pathetic light held first aloft then near the ground. To make certain that Hans, also, had not been tossed from that crashing car.

At last, convinced that Elena alone had perished, Joanne returned, spent, to the road. She reached for the door of her car, swayed, clutched her head, then leaned, retching, over the ditch.

She steadied, eventually, and sat for a while in the car. Forgetful of the flask, she was longing for a drink to remove that acrid taste. Perhaps she could find a stream or a roadside well.

Searching as she drove slowly along, she saw a stone-sided trough against a dry-stone wall. The sound of running water told her its contents should be fresh.

Setting the handbrake, then switching off the ignition, Joanne hurried from the car. She scooped the cool water with her hand, rinsing her mouth three times, then cupping her hand again and again to gulp the soft, icy, liquid.

Standing erect, head high, Joanne breathed deeply of the cleansing hilltop air. No matter that it poured, this was life-restoring. Now she paused, blinked, looked again. Rain had cleared the mist. A field-length away she could just discern a building's silhouette at the end of a rutted track. Some irregularity in its outline indicated it was derelict. And she was investigating every heap of stones that might conceal a man!

She sped down the track, went headlong

over a boulder but staggered, unheeding, to her feet to run stumbling on.

The hinges of the half-rotten door yielding to the second heave from her shoulder, she lunged inside.

She felt paved slabs beneath her feet, raised and flicked her lighter. The flint, wearing down now, produced only an abortive spark. Again she tried, again and yet again. Nothing.

Something reached Joanne's nostrils—the odour, unmistakable, of some human being, confined too long, unwashed.

Desperately, she flicked the lighter, tearing skin from her fingers, and evoked a wan glow.

In the far corner huddled something that looked like a heap of rags—capped by unkempt fair hair.

"Hans!" Forgetting to keep her lighter glowing, Joanne hurtled across.

Her foot caught his outstretched leg, he moaned, flinched, but didn't draw away.

"You're alive!" she yelled, thudding to her knees almost on top of him. "Hans, Hans darling, it's all right," she sobbed; "I've found you, I've found you!"

There was no response.

In the dark, tense silence Joanne wondered

if that initial movement, and the moan, had been only her wishful thinking. She tried to re-ignite her lighter—vainly. She fumbled through the bundled clothing till she found a hand. It was cold . . . ominously cold. Her fingers slid to the wrist—failed to detect the slightest flutter.

"No!" she screamed; "No!" Her voice echoed round the barren walls. He couldn't be dead. She couldn't have come all this way, have found him—too late . . . ?

In panic, Joanne forgot her first aid training, wasting several minutes. Then, panic dulling into the anxiety which seemed a part of her these days, she started reasoning. First, she felt again beneath the layers of clothing—cursing trembling fingers, she un-fastened Hans's shirt, laid her ear against his chest.

There, faintly, was a heart-beat. "Thank God!" she murmured. But how cold he was. Fastening his shirt, she pulled other garments round him, adding her own coat.

Her eyes becoming accustomed to the dark interior, she made out a pile of wood. If only her lighter were functioning she could light a fire; that'd introduce some heat into this place.

It was then Joanne remembered lighting a cigarette from the dashboard lighter in the car. That way she'd get a fire started.

Quickly, she moved the car into the track leading to the ruin. And she found the vacuum flask which she'd forgotten. If Hans recovered consciousness she'd give him soup. It seemed as though he'd gone for days without food, water or heating.

Still inside the car, Joanne collected every kind of paper in sight—certain that the wood, being damp, would need coaxing. Then she lit her cigarette, discovered how she needed something to steady her. Picking up the sandwiches, the flask and pile of paper, she hurried towards the ruined building.

Feverishly she tore up maps and crumpled the newspaper, poking them into spaces in the wood she'd formed into a rough pyramid in the huge fireplace. Then she held her cigarette against the paper.

It flared immediately, and she knew for a time she'd have some light. If the wood ignited she could keep the fire burning through the night. And she *must*—to keep Hans alive. Later, if she was sure he'd survive, she'd go for help. But until he regained consciousness she dared not leave him.

Whoever his captors, they'd provided no essentials. A large plastic bowl, long since dry, lay a short distance from him, together with an enamel mug. On a stone slab rested a plate and fork, nothing more.

Joanne returned to the fire. One thin piece of kindling was alight, thank goodness, crackling, throwing off sparks. She pushed it towards the heart of the pile, hoping it would light the others. And as she watched, thicker timber began to smoulder.

"Don't go out," she pleaded. "Please—don't go out." And she went across to Hans.

He was half-sitting, half-lying in the corner—in what seemed a most ungainly position. One leg was twisted beneath him, the other extended at an angle. Kneeling down, she tried to make him more comfortable. As she touched his right leg he gave an animal-like yelp and shuddered.

"Hans!" she cried, urgently, trying to reach through to his conscious. She gave his shoulder a gentle shake.

His eyelids flickered. His lips parted, struggling to frame a word.

"Elena?"

He was coming round. She mustn't be upset, hurt, because he'd said that woman's name.

"Hans is alive—hang on to that, think of nothing else," she warned herself. "Forget, for now, your trust was misplaced."

Next, Joanne tried, without disturbing him too much, to hold him to her. He must have warmth. Although cold, she was sure there'd be some heat from herself.

His eyes remained closed. She thought he'd lapsed into unconsciousness again, his head against her shoulder. She turned slightly, brushed the prickly cheek with her lips. Against his, she felt the tears on her own face and was surprised.

"Oh, God—let him survive," she prayed, "*please*. No matter if he always wishes Elena had come through with him, let him live . . ."

She began thinking of his mother—thank goodness Frau Lindt couldn't know what her son endured. But once Hans was receiving medical help she'd let her know that he was alive. How relieved she'd be—as would the faithful Mathilde.

Even though she now knew Hans had come away with Elena, a fact she'd be some long while accepting, Joanne would wish to see his mother again. Perhaps he'd understand that desire, wouldn't object to her visiting the chalet.

The fire spluttered, threatening to die. She disentangled herself and went to its rescue. With a stout stick she prodded the embers. A sudden spurt of flame forced her to turn away.

Hans was watching her, slowly shaking his head. "It is a dream . . ." he croaked, "cannot be anything . . . else . . ."

She shook her head, tried to smile but achieved only a tremulous attempt before rushing to him. Carefully avoiding his legs, Joanne dropped to the ground beside him and flung her arms round his neck.

"Oh, Hans, Hans!"

Now she must lose no time, while consciousness remained, before giving him some nourishment.

"I've some soup. It may not be very hot, but we'll see . . ."

The soup was steaming still. She poured a little into the cup and came towards him.

"My hands . . ." he began, sounding alarmed. "I can't feel them . . ."

"Never mind, for now. Drink this—I'll

hold the cup. Then we'll massage life into your hands again."

"Tastes good," Hans commented, after the second cup. "I thought I'd had it, Jo," he added, in that strange, hoarse voice. "I really believed this was the finish."

She took his hands, in turn, chafing them between her own. After what seemed an age he managed to flex his fingers.

"Joanne—how did you find me?"

"That's a long story and you're very weak—it'll keep. Let's concentrate on keeping you alive till I can fetch help."

"I'll survive now, I know that."

"You'd better!" Joanne grinned suddenly, only to frown when Hans groaned as he tried altering his position.

"Your legs—what happened?"

"Broken, I guess—both of them."

"How?"

Hans nodded towards stone steps leading to an upper storey. "They threw me down those. I was upstairs at first—he started knocking me about. I was weak already, had scarcely eaten for days, and because I wouldn't comply . . ."

"With what, Hans? And for whom?"

"The old story—they wanted me to sign

over the Company. When I wouldn't they tried to rough me up."

"Succeeded—by the look of you!"

"Well, I shall not get in much skiing this season."

"But who was it, Hans?"

He stared down, hard, at the hand she was massaging.

"Brace yourself, Joanne—for a shock . . . It was that fellow you knew in Italy—Neville."

"Oh, I know he's involved."

"Then why the blazes encourage him?"

"Steady, don't get upset. I didn't know then—I never suspected a thing till we met over here."

"Met? On purpose . . . ?"

"Neville was—supposedly—helping me find you."

"Like hell!"

"When I was told it all fell into place—how it could have been him arranging the disappearance of the baggage, spreading the news . . . And I was right—I've seen those missing suitcases, at some farm Neville took me to . . ."

"When was this?"

"Yesterday—no, the day before. Oh, so much has happened. But I'm sure we can prove it was him, and that he contrived the attack by that dog on Capri. Remember you said they were hitting at your firm by getting rid of the staff?"

Joanne thought for a minute. "Did you meet up with him after leaving the chalet?"

Hans nodded. "The morning after our engagement party."

How could he even mention that? Joanne felt . . . wooden inside, recalling the evening. Because all the time Hans had been aching for Elena. Why hadn't he been honest? Why, oh why, had he courted *her* so convincingly?

Joanne realized he'd have to know, some time, about the smashed Lancia—about Elena. Could she bring herself to tell him? It'd be unwise yet to convey such awful news, she decided—and recognized that as a welcome excuse.

Until she saw his grief, she might continue fooling herself that having found Hans everything would be all right.

Restless, Joanne went to prod, needlessly, at the fire. "I'm going for help now," she announced, over her shoulder. "You're fit to be left—briefly—and it's high time you had medical attention."

"Not yet," Hans protested. "Wait till morning. Don't leave me, Jo."

Don't call me that! she longed to scream. "Jo" belongs to the good days, when you loved me.

"Please, Joanne, don't go till daylight."

"It's best. Besides, I must inform the police where you are—I meant to tell them where I was heading and never did . . . Then I'll let your mother know, and the Company."

"They can wait. I need you, Jo."

She wouldn't look at him. She had to get out of here, for a while—get away from him. *From Hans*, this man who'd been restored . . . but not to *her*. Because Elena might be dead, but she'd live on, she was a part of Hans.

Joanne reached the doorway, against which she'd leaned the splintered door. It took time moving it aside. "I won't be long . . ."

"Joanne, I beg you—stay."

Slowly, she turned, went with every step heavy towards that far corner. She gave an awkward shrug.

"Any soup left?" Hans enquired.

"A little." She picked up the flask. "There are sandwiches also, if you can manage them."

She held out the cup.

Hans patted the ground beside him, moved his covering so the slabs weren't bare. "Sit here, please."

Joanne hesitated.

Hans grinned ruefully. "I know—I'm filthy. Don't know when I last washed but . . . I'm sorry, Jo."

"It's not that; though I'll clean you up soon—didn't want to bother you before."

She sat beside him. And knew it was useless contemplating visiting the chalet again—ever. Being with Hans and knowing he was in love with somebody else was . . . intolerable. Think of something different, she told herself silently; talk of *anything*.

"Your legs—how long since they were injured?"

"Lord knows! In the early days. I lost all track of time, they took my watch."

"I know. It was sent to our Berne office, with the second ransom demand."

"Ransom? What were they after?"

Joanne told him the sum, ". . . and surrender of your Company."

"Thank God they held out." Hans paused, reflecting. "And Mother . . . knew all this?"

"It was better than believing you dead."

"The bastards!"

Joanne began cleaning him up as best she could—with water she fetched from the roadside well.

She wondered about attending to his legs but since the injuries were old now, she decided to leave first aid to the ambulance men.

Once Hans was more comfortable, Joanne settled beside him to wait for the morning.

★   ★   ★

Hans had slept off and on throughout the night. But she had remained rigid, reflecting on events since fate's ironic twist brought them together. Almost, she wished now she'd never taken the job . . . Except—well, she had reached Hans. She believed he'd survive now.

He stirred as she rose to build up the fire before leaving to seek a telephone. Observing light filtering in through broken panes, he smiled slightly. "I'll be fine now, Jo—you do what you have to. Is there a call box nearby? I was blindfolded when they brought me."

"There's a farm quite near, if they're on

the phone I should be away only a matter of minutes."

Hans nodded.

"I'd beg a hot drink from them and something for you to eat, but you'd better have nothing more till the hospital people see you. If they need to administer an anaesthetic for setting those legs, they won't thank me for giving you food and causing further delay."

"Whatever you say."

Hans appeared remarkably rational for somebody who had endured acute pain whilst facing gradual starvation. She would never forget the inner strength this disclosed. Even when she no longer saw Hans she'd continue to esteem him. Indeed, she knew she'd always remember the many fine qualities which had drawn her to him.

She sighed and made a sudden dash for the door.

"Joanne . . ."

"Yes?" She just stood there, not even turning to look at him.

"Bless you for all you've done—for that dogged persistence which led to finding me. I don't know when we'll manage a private word again—come back here, Joanne; I owe you so much . . ."

But she ran outside, calling over her shoulder, "Later, Hans. I must ring for an ambulance."

Inside the car, she remembered the revolver and ammunition. Hans needed some protection. She made herself return to him. "Here . . ." she began, "this gun was in the car. You'd better have it—just in case."

As she leaned over, Hans caught her sleeve, trying to pull her nearer. "Darling, I haven't even said 'hallo' properly—give me a chance."

But Joanne was determined on keeping him at arm's length. If he loved Elena, his gratitude was no compensation.

The effort paining his legs, Hans moaned and slipped back to rest his head, wearily, against the damp wall. But he had her by the arm still, and raised her hand to his lips.

Her eyes misted again, but she wriggled her hand free of his. "Shan't be long," she muttered, avoiding his eyes which she knew were bewildered, reproachful. Why was he so insensitive—expecting her to act out this charade—knowing his first conscious thought had been for Elena?

She started the car and reversed up the track to the road. Minutes later she was knocking on the door of a house from which she'd heard laughter last night. A smiling middle-aged woman answered.

"Yes, love, what is it?"

"I wondered—do you have a telephone?"

"Aye, that's right—are you wanting to use it?"

"If you don't mind," she hesitated, not wishing to say too much. "My friend's had a slight accident, I want to call an ambulance and the police—if that's okay."

She asked the farm's exact location, pinpointing the spot for the ambulance. And then she contacted the police.

With what she hoped was fitting tact, Joanne cut short the woman's concerned questioning and dashed out to the car. She must get back to Hans—at once. Instead of the relief she'd expected on summoning help, she had a premonition of imminent disaster.

She flung herself into the driving seat, started the engine, and accelerated towards Hans's hideout.

The end of the cart track was coming into sight when her mirror revealed a car gaining on her at fantastic speed. As it approached she slowed instinctively, to let it pass. But the driver cut in, almost scraping her bonnet.

Fuming, Joanne wondered what the fellow was about. Then he turned left, sharply, towards the ruined house.

Momentarily, Joanne wondered if this was the police, although she doubted that they'd arrive this quickly.

She followed and found the other car broadside on. She was reflecting that it must have skidded when Neville sprang from the driver's seat. He strode to Joanne's door, even before her sharp stab at the brake pedal halted the car completely.

"Move over," he snapped.

As he opened her door, she could hear the agitated impatience of his breathing. As she reached the passenger seat he was sitting next to her. "Just in time—another second and you'd have been in that place." He nodded towards the ruin. "I'll tell you what you'd have found—your friend, Hans Lindt; whether alive or dead is anyone's guess!"

Joanne made her face impassive—Neville mustn't suspect that she'd been inside already, that help was on its way. She must delay him . . . But how? How *could* she; limbs trembling, heart pounding . . . ? If only he'd been later, five minutes might have sufficed, so that she wouldn't have had to fight, alone—for Hans, for her own life.

"You're clever, Joanne—too clever for your own good. I don't know how you traced your boy-friend here, but I've got to hand it to you—you're not stupid." Smiling oddly, Neville jerked her towards him, turning her so she was half on the floor over the gear lever, her head against the dashboard. "How does it feel?" he demanded, "knowing you're so close to him, yet you didn't quite make it?" Suddenly he struck her head, for emphasis, against the car. "Because you won't win! I'm going to finish you off—as I should have done long since!" Again, he banged down with her head and Joanne felt the warm, sticky trickle down her neck, from the gashes induced by the dashboard.

"Don't worry, not much longer . . ." Neville declared. He had a handful of her hair in his restraining grasp now, while with the other hand he explored first the glove compartment then the parcel shelf. For the revolver.

Her eyes held wide open by his grip on her hair, she saw his puzzled frown but knew it would only be a matter of moments before he found other ways of killing her. And one was bound to succeed—he'd stop at nothing now.

His hands slid to her throat, started choking the life from her before she was even aware of his intention. But Joanne couldn't just let this happen. Maybe life had seemed a dismal prospect since her future with Hans had disintegrated, but it was *her life* still, she'd fight for its continuance.

Her hands had gone instinctively, fruitlessly, to his forearms, now she moved them, swiftly. She rendered Neville an almighty thump in his groin whilst she thrust the other index finger and thumb sharply up his nostrils—until he yelled.

Releasing her instantly, Neville shot a hand to each area of pain. Joanne pressed hard on the car horn.

Recovering slightly, Neville straightened in his seat. He must have opted for a fight out in the open—he wrestled with the car door then half-stepped, half-fell out on to the track. He tried to pull Joanne with him but she clung to the steering column, using it as leverage. If he dragged her arm from its socket, she'd not follow him.

Again, Joanne located the horn and gave a long blast.

All at once there was a sharp retort, followed swiftly by a second. Neville slumped, clutching the pit of his stomach and his leg.

She stared, disbelievingly, at the dark stains creeping through his light trousers, and watched him writhe before he rolled over on the ground. He appeared to lose consciousness.

Joanne eased herself out of her awkward position across the front seats of the car. Standing, she noticed the shakiness of her legs and the throbbing starting up in her skull. She struggled past the car and wove a meandering way towards the other vehicle blocking her path.

In her shocked state it wasn't easy scrambling between that and the ruined house but there was just sufficient room to get by. She staggered the last few paces to the door.

Grinning, Hans lay on his stomach in the doorway—still holding the gun. "Thank God you warmed the numbness from my fingers!" he exclaimed, then as she knelt beside him he continued anxiously, "Are you all right, *Liebchen*?"

Speechlessly, she nodded, trying to find

some words, however inadequate, to thank him; but nothing would come. And before she could even move a hand in a grateful gesture, the clanging bell announced the ambulance.

From the doorway, Joanne observed the driver's amazement as he took in the fact that *two* injured men required attention.

"Dare I hope you've called the police as well?" the ambulanceman asked, after hearing out her rapid explanation of Neville's wounds. Joanne reassured him that she had, and helped move the two cars so that the ambulance could be brought farther down the track.

Swiftly, Hans and Neville were carried into the vehicle. The driver was arranging that Joanne would ride with them to the hospital when the police arrived.

She gave them a brief resumé of developments since her phone call to them before being helped into the police car to travel in convoy with the ambulance.

★   ★   ★

Joanne shivered as she walked along the

333

hospital corridor—a shiver unconnected with the temperature.

Her gashed head had been stitched and dressed and she had telephoned Wilhelm Schmidt and Frau Lindt. Both of them had, of course, been ecstatic on learning of Hans's release, although to his mother Joanne had had to play down the extent of his injuries.

She had spent some time with the police and seemed to have satisfied them with her statement. And so now she could find nothing else with which to defer the awful moment when she must see Hans and break to him the news of Elena's death.

Earlier, Joanne had asked his doctors if he was fit to receive upsetting news. But if she'd hoped concern for his health would excuse her leaving the wretched job in abeyance she'd been wrong.

The young houseman had smiled. "He's come through the ordeal extremely well—he should stand up to that," he told her when she'd revealed the nature of the news. "After all," he'd added—rather unfeelingly, she'd thought—"he's in the right spot for sedation if he's distraught."

Hans had been bathed *and* shaved so, despite the contraption now supporting his injured legs, he looked substantially the same person she'd known and loved for what now seemed a very long time. Colour was returning to his cheeks and his eyes lit up as Joanne walked into the side ward which he occupied.

She meant to ignore his extended hand, but found herself taking it as she sat beside the bed. "How are you?" Her own voice sounded strange round the lump which seemed, these days, to be a permanency in her throat.

"I am fine, darling, thank you," Hans reassured her. "I wish you looked brighter! That fellow must have given you a bad fright. Come on, Jo—we'll both survive now. And immediately I am out of here we shall put this behind us and get . . ."

"I'll never be able to tell you how grateful I am," she interrupted before he could continue his facile plans for their future—a future which, she was certain, he'd no wish to realize.

Hans chuckled. "Oh, you will—there will be all the time in the world. And I shall enjoy hearing how marvellous you think I am, simply because I was once taught how to use a gun! But you know, Joanne, this is all unnecessary—we are quits. I would not have lasted much longer in that place, if you had not arrived."

"Hans, listen to me," Joanne insisted urgently, fixing her gaze on the rails above his bed—avoiding the sorrow which she knew she'd bring to his eyes. "Prepare yourself for a shock, Hans—a bad one."

"Mother?"

"No. No, she's . . . as well as one can expect. I rang her—she sends her love." Get on with it, Joanne, she told herself. Get it over, then you can turn and run. You needn't wait to see his hurt . . .

"Kurt then—what's happened to him?"

"Nothing, he's all right. It's worse than that, Hans . . ."

"But *you* are here, *Liebchen*, alive and . . ."

"Hans, do listen!" She was shouting and shouldn't be, in hospital. Any minute they'd send her away. She'd got to tell him first.

"It's Elena—there was an accident. She's dead . . ." Joanne's voice trailed off. She couldn't continue driving stakes into the heart of this man she loved. Nor could she find words to say she was sorry about Elena.

"I see. And . . . ?" Hans sounded curiously unmoved.

"That's it—she's . . ." She couldn't bring herself to repeat the word.

"I heard you the first time, Joanne. I do not know what reaction you expect, but I cannot pretend . . ."

"You needn't," she managed, marvelling at his composure. "I'm going now." Thankful that she could finally do just that, she stood up.

"Like hell you are! Sit down." His sharp tone made Joanne look at him at last. "*Liebchen*, what is it?" Hans persisted. And there was only concern for her in those blue eyes—no hint of distress.

"It's just strain—having to break the news to you."

Why were his calm eyes declaring he'd felt nothing for Elena?

"After all," Joanne continued, "it was her name you called when you regained consciousness."

"Well, how could I have anticipated the miracle that brought you to me? All I knew was that she'd gone out for provisions—one, maybe two, days previously—and had not returned."

"So she was with you." Even though Joanne had felt certain of this since he'd spoken Elena's name, she'd not yet completely accepted the fact.

"Yes. I thought you understood that . . ."

Joanne nodded, looked away. "Was—was she helping you escape?"

"You have to be joking!"

She glanced quickly at Hans.

"Elena was on their side, Jo—haven't you put two and two together?"

"You mean . . . ? But Neville said . . ."

"And you believed him?"

"Well—no. But when I learned she'd been here with you . . ."

"Now you listen to me, little lady," Hans continued, his voice infinitely more severe than his twinkling eyes, "instead of to that wheeler-dealer who links names indiscriminately to serve his ends! However, *Neville* is not your problem. And you should not let Elena upset you. She would be gloating now, if she was anywhere where the soul lingers . . ."

"Hans!"

"Do not admonish me about respect for the dead! She was evil, Joanne—I always suspected that. The way she shifted to the opposition was proof enough."

"She did what . . . ?" Joanne could not

grasp the full implication of what Hans was saying.

"Elena was determined to get her hands on the Company. She had accepted that you and I would marry, thus cutting out one possible means to her end, when Neville contacted her. Later, she actually boasted to me that he'd eagerly sought her co-operation. His bait, a seat on the new Company board, was sufficient persuasion for her."

"But how could she help him?"

"Haven't you connected? First, the accident in Florence—with me out of the way, she would have been the majority shareholder. Or *Kurt*, under her control. She and Neville would have had a free hand. "

"I see."

"When the accident didn't quite come off as planned, they decided on the kidnap attempt. I did not realize until you told me, that they were holding me hostage—I thought they only meant to ensure I remained missing until I either died, or my death was legally presumed."

"But why, Hans—why was your company threatened, why *you*?"

"Greed!"

"Oh."

"I told you about that rival's bid for my Company. I can only assume the attendant publicity alerted someone to the profit being made by a good travel firm. I believe their original intention was to blacken our image within the business, enabling some competitor to win over our clients. Hence the numerous accidents, injuries to staff, disappearances of baggage. At that stage, Neville was probably merely a link-man. But he grew ambitious. He wanted me out of the business so *he* could take over. And so unpleasantness became . . . violence. It is a relief it is ended; I had to be so wary that I could not take even our newest courier on trust—you recall?"

Joanne nodded. "And are you saying they *forced* you away from home that morning?"

"No. That was Elena—again. She found one of the few reasons that would draw me— Kurt. She swore he was ill, swathed in blankets in the car; ready to dash to hospital. She seemed distraught, begged me to go with her. When I went to look at the boy, she pulled me away, saying he was sleeping at last, must not be disturbed. We went tearing over the mountain pass, I've never known her drive so fast. It was only as day broke that a further glance to the bundle of covers on the back seat made me sense something was wrong. And I suggested again that we should take a look at Kurt."

Hans paused, smiling ruefully, then went on. "Something in her expression told me I had been a gullible idiot to take her word. My only excuse was that I was not feeling over-bright. I had had only a few hours' sleep after our party, and then been awakened suddenly."

"What did Elena do when she learned you were on to her?"

"She drove even faster—possibly knowing I'd never attempt to leap from the car at that speed. Then soon we made the rendezvous with Neville. He was armed—so was Elena, come to that. The rest of the journey was at gun-point. Our destination was some private air-strip, I'm not even sure where. We took off in an ancient freight transporter . . ."

"I see—to avoid routine airport checks which would have revealed that they were armed . . ."

Hans nodded. "I suppose so—never thought of that, but I had more to occupy me. Such as how to get away, when I daren't risk a scuffle in flight. I know what a gun can do, going off in an aircraft."

"And then you touched down over here?"

"Somewhere, yes. I was blindfolded then. It must have been another private airfield, there were no controls of any kind. Elena brought me here by car—the rest you know."

"And she guarded you?"

"Precisely, and on occasions Neville joined her."

"In between meeting me in Italy, kidding me along he was *helping*. Lord, was I stupid!"

"But he was convincing . . ."

"Did he convince *you*—or did you suspect him all along?"

"Well, I always had a shrewd idea he was involved. He knew a hell of a lot about our Company schedules. I hoped if I concealed my doubts he would ultimately give himself away. Only by then he was paying you attention—and you seemed oblivious to my warnings. I became terrified for your safety—I was quite relieved when I was the one taken captive, thinking I'd drawn Neville from you. But then he left Elena in charge."

"Did she keep you covered the whole time?"

"Until they did this to my legs—then I couldn't give anyone much trouble. It seems they had my measure!"

"Until you pulled the gun on Neville today."

Hans grinned. "Ah, well—it was you in danger then, I . . . sort of forgot about a couple of useless legs." His grin widened. "Just so long as you don't expect me to grovel along the ground for you ever again! Once I'm out of this unaccustomed prone position, I shall soon be in charge again."

". . . of me?" Joanne asked mischievously.

Hans shrugged. "I doubt that—you appear to have found untold resources whilst hounding me out. I am not at all sure I can cope with you!"

Joanne smiled—the first real smile for too long, and leaned towards him. "Maybe I'll make it easy for you—meet you half-way."

Hans smiled back, wryly. "You will have to, for a time at least, I can make no move towards you!"

She leaned closer still until his lips claimed hers. As the kiss ended his eyes, suddenly grave, met hers. Their glance held and Joanne knew that she'd never again question that Hans needed her.

He laughed, ruefully, indicating his injured legs. "Not exactly a good start, is it—for *us*?"

Joanne shrugged. "That's life . . . !"

"Yes, I'm afraid it is—there's always something wrong."

Her hand tightened on his. "But more that's . . . right."

Hans smiled. "Oh, absolutely!"

THE END